S0-ABO-658

Change
of
Heart

Change
of
Heart

Enjoy the adventure!
God Bless You
Carmen Peone

Carmen Peone

TATE PUBLISHING & *Enterprises*

Change of Heart
Copyright © 2011 by Carmen Peone. All rights reserved.

No part of this publication may be reproduced, stored in a retrieval system or transmitted in any way by any means, electronic, mechanical, photocopy, recording or otherwise without the prior permission of the author except as provided by USA copyright law.

This novel is a work of fiction. Names, descriptions, entities, and incidents included in the story are products of the author's imagination. Any resemblance to actual persons, events, and entities is entirely coincidental.

The opinions expressed by the author are not necessarily those of Tate Publishing, LLC.

Published by Tate Publishing & Enterprises, LLC
127 E. Trade Center Terrace | Mustang, Oklahoma 73064 USA
1.888.361.9473 | www.tatepublishing.com

Tate Publishing is committed to excellence in the publishing industry. The company reflects the philosophy established by the founders, based on Psalm 68:11,
"The Lord gave the word and great was the company of those who published it."

Book design copyright © 2011 by Tate Publishing, LLC. All rights reserved.
Cover design by Jeff Fisher
Interior design by Joel Uber

Published in the United States of America

ISBN: 978-1-61739-335-8
1. Fiction; Christian, Suspense
2. Fiction; Cultural Heritage
11.01.26

Dedication

For my son Marshall who always believed in me.
I love you! In memory of Marguerite Ensminger, thank
you for sharing your language with me.

Acknowledgements

Thank you to my husband Joe, our sons, Corey, Cody and Eddy, and Becky England for your everlasting support on this journey.

Arrow Lakes
Language Sound Guide

The <u>K</u> is a guttural K sound which is used deep in the throat.

The "who" is a soft blowing sound, not the word who.

The <u>huh</u> is a sound that comes from the back of the throat, as if one has something stuck in the back of the throat and is trying to get it out.

The <u>lth</u> sound is a lisping sound when the tongue is placed behind the front teeth and one blows softly.

The ch sound is a sharp ch not a soft ch sound.

The "K" with no bar is a soft k sound.

Chapter 1

The lodge flap flipped open and *Hamis-hamis*, ("Morning Dove") burst inside. Her face was crimson and her eyes looked wild.

"*Spupaleena* ("Rabbit"), what are you doing?" she clenched her jaw.

"What do you mean?" Spupaleena, a typical thirteen-year-old, was enjoying the brisk morning with a cup of rosehip tea. She sat on her tule-mat by the fire daydreaming. She had no idea why her *lthkickha* ("Older Sister") was so heated. All of her morning chores were finished and she was merely taking a break, enjoying the colors of the fire.

"I have been searching the village for you." Hamis-hamis swiped the sweat trickling down her brow. "Don't tell me you're just waking up!" Hamis-hamis's eyes sparked with anger; she stood with her hands set on her hips. "The day's half over and there's work to be done. It's starting to snow again—"

"I've been up for a while now if it's any of your concern." Spupaleena shook her head in irritation.

"What do you really want? Or, did you come here just to hear your own words?" Spupaleena scrambled to her feet and faced her <u>lth</u>kickha. She looked lean and strong. Her long legs carried her lanky frame with a sense of grace and courage.

"*Tima* ("Grandmother") needs my help right now, so you have to watch *Pekam* ("Bobcat") today." Hamis-hamis stared at Spupaleena as a mother does to her naughty child.

"I can't. *Mistum* ("Father") is showing me his new snare lines when he returns from the morning hunt." Spupaleena, flashed her <u>lth</u>kickha a look of disgust. "You can easily watch over Pekam and cook too." She decided that today she would not cower to Hamis-hamis as she had done all her life.

It was time to take a stand. Since their mother's death, Spupaleena felt that her sister thought she needed to take that role upon herself. Hamis-hamis was older, taller, and thicker than she, but Spupaleena was ready. She was sick of being bossed around day after day. She thought, *I am thirteen, a woman. I should not be treated as a child.*

"Besides," said Spupaleena, "you are not my *toom* ("Mother"), and can't give me orders." She clenched her fists in rage.

Ka kee cha na ("Chickadee"), the kids' mother, had died a few years ago from a cougar attack while picking huckleberries deep in the mountains. The girls had been close by and witnessed the attack and death of their beloved toom. They had never been the same since the horrific mauling.

Hamis-hamis reached for her birch broom. She shoved the broom in front of her lthkickha.

"I think you need a lesson in manners. You still haven't learned much respect these days, *chuchoops* ("Little Sister")," Hamis-hamis's face reddened with each breath. She trembled with fear as Spupaleena had never challenged her before. But Hamis-hamis knew the situation would only get worse if her bluff was called. "You are just a silly little girl who thinks running after mistum's pelts is important work. There's much to be done around here and you always seem to skip out in order to play with your animals, dead or alive. We all have to work. We all have to help. You are lazy and no good. I wish you would have died and mother would have lived."

Spupaleena gasped. The sister's gazes locked before Spupaleena made her move. She was not only sick and tired of Hamis-hamis's self-righteousness, but was now infuriated with her cruelty. She had endured her sister's dark words all these years to avoid upsetting her beloved *stimteema* ("Grandmother"), *Sneena*("Owl"), who was old and frail. Spupaleena was sure that any turmoil would bring her precious tima to her grave.

"You'll never talk to me like that again! I'm sick of your criticism and sick of you badgering me day after day. It's over! I've had all I can take from you. You make me sick!" Spupaleena gathered her courage and stood her ground.

"What did you say?"

"I said you make me sick!" Spupaleena found a confidence she had never known. "You think you can boss me around like I'm your servant girl. You pretend to do your chores, but I see you walking around the village whispering lies—"

"Is that what you think? Chuchoops, here's your lesson in manners!"

Hamis-hamis swung her broom with all her might. Spupaleena jerked to the side, but not quick enough. The broom handle caught her on the cheek. Blood ran from the wound, but Spupaleena felt nothing. She grabbed the tattered broom from Hamis-hamis's hands, throwing it in the popping fire. Her fury dulled any sense of pain. Her rationale left as quickly as her patience.

"You will never touch me again," Spupaleena shouted. She pushed her sister so hard that Hamis-hamis fell out of the flap of their six-foot pit dwelling and into the snow. Spupaleena grabbed her elk robe from her tule-mat bed and sprinted out the hide door.

Spupaleena ran. She had no idea where she was headed. She just ran. Hot tears stung her eyes in the cold, cruel wind as they streamed down her frozen face.

Her mind was racing so fast that no thought stuck. Spupaleena did not understand what she could have done to capture her sister's wrath. *Why did Hamis-hamis try to harm me?* she thought.

Her anguish drove her to keep moving forward in the pelting snow and wind. She would half run and half hop a few yards and fall. She told herself, *Get up and press on.* Spupaleena squinted through the blinding snow. Her face felt like tiny needles; she knew numbness would follow. She wished she would have thought to grab her snowshoes. Travel would have been much quicker. Her long legs sank down past her knees with each step slowing her pace.

Spupaleena stopped. She bent over with her arms across her stomach, gasping for air. The cold rushed into her lungs, burning with each breath. Dropping to her knees, she looked to the heavens and cried out to the Creator for answers. She sobbed and screamed. She released an exasperated sigh. Her body shook not of cold, but of raw emotion. She was too exhausted to go any further. Sitting back on her feet, she curled herself forward. Defeat taunted Spupaleena as she cupped her face in her hands and cried until she had nothing left.

A screen of white snowflakes surrounded her as she sat, staring into nothingness. She failed to notice the whirling wind swirling her long, thick hair around in the frigid air. Spupaleena could neither think nor feel. The snow piled on top of her elk robe. After some time, Spupaleena rose and began walking again. Her feet and legs wobbled, hardly able to carry her. She swayed like an old larch tree in the wind.

Spupaleena had been wandering for nearly an hour before she finally stopped. Looking around, nothing seemed familiar; all she could see was a white screen. The snowflakes seemed to be the size of wild rose petals and they now dropped down in a thick-pelting sheet. "I must keep going," she whispered. She could hear her father's voice telling her to, *be prepared for the worst.*

She tried to focus on the last elk hunt she took with her father. He taught her the exact spot to land an arrow to instantly kill an elk and how to prepare the carcass so the meat would not spoil. The voice came again, *be prepared.* She stumbled around, trying to focus on her father's teachings. Her mistum had always been her hero.

"I need to stay awake. I need to remember how mistum set the rabbit snare…" she mumbled. Her body shook with fear and cold. "I was taught well, I can…I can…I…" she sighed.

Spupaleena fell to her knees. Her breath came quickly; she could barely keep her eyes open. Memories faded in and out. However, one hung on tightly. She focused on one of her favorite times of the year: the *in-tee-tee-huh* ("Salmon") runs that took place every spring at the Kettle Falls on the Columbia River that she visited with her family. She could see her dad standing out on the wooden platform with his net. She saw him scooping up a ninety-pound salmon

Carmen Peone

with little effort. She could almost smell the churning water and fresh salmon. These adventures with him built confidence in her ability to survive, and that time was now upon her.

Scanning the area, Spupaleena knew she needed to find shelter. Darkness was coming quickly and the snow had no intentions of letting up. She stood and glanced around. Spupaleena knew she had to continue the search for a fir tree with branches close to the ground. She took a handful of snow and put it in her mouth to replenish the fluids throughout her body. She wrapped her elk robe tightly around her body and went on her way.

She located a cluster of trees a few yards away and scraped the snow from under one of them as best she could; it was especially difficult only having her hands and feet to work with. Once she was satisfied with the beginnings of her pit, she set out to find branches low enough to snap off and gather for the warmth of a lean-to.

She only found a handful of branches and laid them on the floor of her makeshift shelter. Much more was needed if she was to wait the night out and not freeze. It was much colder now than the previous day and she questioned whether or not her elk robe would be sufficient. She had no knife and knew it would be a struggle to gather the boughs. She was becoming weaker as the day progressed.

Spupaleena's fingers were red and swollen. She could faintly feel her toes and feet. Exhaustion was beating her down, however, she knew to persevere, to stay awake, and finish her task. She had to survive, no matter what. She had to go on and prepare for the worst, because the worst was looking her in the face. Her father had given her the gift of knowledge; now it was up to her to do what had been engraved in her mind.

She missed her mistum. She longed for his warmth and love. Spupaleena knew he would be worried. She hated herself for that. *Skumhist* ("Black Bear") should not have to agonize over his run-away daughter. He was strong and worked hard for his family. If anything, she would succeed for him and him alone.

"Back to work," she said with determination.

Spupaleena scavenged the area for usable boughs. She found several full, thick branches that would frame and fill in the lean-to nicely. She scooped up another handful of snow and ate it before packing the wood back. Standing over her spread-out selection, she nodded her head with approval. She grabbed a third handful of snow and let it melt in her mouth. The coolness seemed to revive her, if only for a short time.

As Spupaleena worked to build her shelter, she tiredly hummed traditional lullabies, and again thought about her time fishing in the early mornings with her mistum. She cherished her time at the large falls. The men would set out their fish nets at sunrise during the summer months, while the women prepared to sun-dry each harvest.

She would watch as Skumhist would walk carefully onto the scaffold and dip his massive net into the churning falls. When he pulled out his net, his eyes would dance with pride. His howls of excitement had been drown out by the crashing of the water pouring over the falls, but she understood his joy. She could feel her own adrenaline rush throughout her body.

Spupaleena snapped out of her daydream. Her cheeks were wet and cold. She wiped away a tear as she sat huddled in her elk robe. She peeked out and blinked away the snowflakes now gently falling against her eyelashes.

The reality of her actions made her sick. The more she thought, the worse she felt. She asked herself, *Could I ever go back? Would my family accept me back after running away?* She had made such a scene.

"No!" she shouted. "I must get away from Hamishamis. I need to start a new life." She tossed a branch into the snow and groaned. "I'm so confused." She sat a while trying to sort out her feelings. One minute, she felt like she could conquer the world; the next, her stomach was all tied up in knots. She knew her emotions merely lied. Truth and reason would need to be her guide, her North Star.

She decided that someday she would see her family again, when the time was right. "I will hold my tima and mistum," she told herself. She held her knees and rocked back and forth trying not to let guilt win her over. *My little brother is too young and won't remember this*, she thought. She sat and soothed herself for a few minutes.

"I need a few more boughs," she said. Still weary and weak, she stood and stretched a bit as her muscles were stiff and sore. She then headed out in search for more fir trees. She meandered for a few yards and then suddenly, she tripped over fallen logs hidden by fresh snow. She rolled down a steep rocky ridge and slammed against two-foot boulders lining a creek bed.

Her body was twisted and her limbs were sprawled out in opposite directions. Spupaleena was stunned. Her mind went blank and her vision was a blur. She just laid there in a fog.

She tried to move, but could only scream in pain, grabbing her right leg. She had never felt pain as intense and sharp as this. She could hardly catch a breath. Her head throbbed as if a hatchet had split right through it. Her sides felt like they were being ripped open with each breath. She was dizzy and her body shook uncontrollably.

Spupaleena lay back in the snow, groaning and gasping for air, tears streaming down the sides of her face. In a matter of seconds, everything went dark and quiet. She lay on the ground as the snow covered up her broken, mangled body.

Carmen Peone

Chapter 2

The morning sun peered through the clouds, catching Spupaleena's attention. She winced, quickly shutting her eyes. She caught her breath as a searing pain stabbed at every nerve in her head. She rolled over and threw up, entertaining death to end the suffering. Her arms and legs were on fire. For a minute, she was unaware of her surroundings and her accident. She twisted from the jolt of electricity running throughout her body. She tried not to move, even breathing was a struggle.

The woods were still, hauntingly quiet. No crunching of tiny feet on the fresh snow. No birds announcing the morning. Spupaleena noticed how warm her buckskin dress and moccasins felt. She was entangled in her elk robe, almost bound like a baby, but was thankful for the warmth it supplied. She could not believe she was still breathing.

Spupaleena recalled grabbing her elk robe and flying out the flap door. Then she remembered. She could hear Hamis-hamis plowing into her intimate morning with a tongue of fire, shouting orders and demanding that she care for Pekam, her precious little brother.

Spupaleena tried to pull herself together and not cry. She cringed at the pain that electrified her body. She gasped with each breath, tilted her head to the side, and vomited again. She rolled back over in the warmth of her elk robe, wishing she had some of the fir boughs to toss on top of her for added protection. She knew she needed as much body heat retained as possible as the snow continued to fall and swirl about. "Thank you, Creator," she whispered. She was thankful to be alive.

She hoped the Creator would give her another day. The air was cold and crisp, threatening to send frosted chills deep into her bones. She prayed her elk robe would indeed keep her body warm enough until she could figure a way out. Her eyelids were so heavy, she allowed them to close. Once again the tears trickled down her cheeks.

When she woke up, the sun had dropped behind the trees and the shadows brought in the frigid air. Most of the day, she came in and out of a fitful sleep. During the moments she was awake, Spupaleena tried to recall the medicines her tima had taught to her. *Alder is for pain and Salmon Berry is for cuts*, she thought. *Was that right?*

Carmen Peone

"What are they?" she winced at the pain that shot down her sides and leg. She was just too groggy to try to remember the herbs.

What she did recall were the times of picking and drying berries and roots for food and medicine. The memories flooded her suddenly. Those were good days for the women of her village. Stories were told and laughter filled the forests. She felt so alone as she reflected on those times with her family.

Spupaleena also remembered the beautifully woven baskets made of cedar bark, and decorated with deep hues of sedge grass and bone beads that stored food and medicines. She began to relax and let her thoughts flow that evening. For a moment, her pain was forgotten as each image presented itself to her. Then sleep came once again and stole away those precious memories. She did, however, sleep dreamless and deep.

The next morning proved cold. The snow grew by inches and the wind howled an eerie call through whipping trees. Spupaleena squinted, trying to keep the wind and snow out of her eyes. Hunger pangs were reminders that she had not eaten for over twenty-four hours and her mouth was dry. She tried to reach for a bit of snow, but failed. The pain in her body was too intense. She was quickly weakening from lack of food and water. Her thoughts were becoming scrambled and unclear.

Spupaleena tried to stay awake. She mulled over the morning she fought with Hamis-hamis. She had been sitting quietly by the fire in her six-foot pit dwelling wondering where everyone was. It was quiet. The air was cold, but still. The popping of the fire was soothing on such a frigid morning, as was the sweet smell of her rosehip tea. She vaguely remembered gazing into the fire dreaming of a peaceful place. She had dreamed of green grasses and rushing streams. As Spupaleena began to cook the morning meal, she sang a lullaby her tima taught to her from before she took her first steps. She recalls rocking back and forth, closing her eyes, and feeling the rhythm of the song. When she finished singing, Spupaleena let the tears roll down her soft cheeks as she realized the world she dreamed of could never be her reality again.

At this point, Spupaleena felt that she might not survive. Doubt was festering into panic. She was busted up and bruised across her face and down her sides. Not only was she famished, she was weak and vulnerable. She could barely lift her head. Just as Hamis-hamis told her, she was just a little, spoiled child.

"*Loot* ("No")!" she said, shattering the stream of fear. "Hamis-hamis is wrong. I will make it; I will live." The muscles in her jaw tightened.

If only someone came looking for me…mistum must be looking for me, she thought.

"*Kunheet incha, kunheet incha* ("Help me, Help me")," she moaned. Exhaustion consumed her and the stabbing pain in her head and throughout her body was more than she could handle.

Finally, unconsciousness came upon her like a rushing creek. As she slept, the snow floated from the sky and landed on her inch by inch. Her breathing was deep and steady. Her dreams became still and her blood flowed slower and slower.

The sound of footsteps roused Spupaleena. She could not muster the strength to open her eyes, but she could vaguely hear the crunching of snow. She groaned as the electrifying pain ran up and down her insides. Her bones felt like they had been sawed into pieces like a hundred broken branches scattered across the ground.

"Are ya alright?" she heard the man say. His voice was quiet and soothing. There was no answer. He felt her pulse.

"Yes, okay…she's alive," he whispered. "Can ya hear me?" he asked again, a little louder this time.

There again was no answer. Spupaleena knew she heard a voice, but she had trouble deciphering the meaning. *I'm here, alive*, she thought.

She felt her entire body throb as someone moved her. The pain was so ruthless that she grabbed her elk robe while every muscle in her body became tense. She groaned in anguish.

She faded in and out for several hours. The excruciating pain made her delirious. Her face was numb and she was exhausted. She had heard a man's voice, but still could not make out the words. The voice sounded the same as before; there must be only one of them. There was something familiar, but she failed to place it. Her head pounded and she was in no shape to think. Her energy was depleted.

"Whoa now, that's it," the man said, waking Spupaleena out of a fitful sleep. She managed to open her eyes, but everything was just a blur. She shut them tightly and tried to lie as quietly as she could. She felt no movement. She did, however, smell something familiar. A few minutes passed when she could hear a woman's voice. It was soft and muffled. The two of them were talking. She knew the words were not of her own people. But the words sounded so familiar. Spupaleena felt the pole structure she was on rock back and forth. The movement was as gentle as could be, but the sharpness intensified, causing her to throw up. She cried out in agony and her head spun. She felt herself being hoisted up and carried. At this instant, she could care less where; she just wanted it all to end. The pain thrust her into unconsciousness.

Chapter 3

Spupaleena looked so peaceful lying in the bed. Her long, tangled hair draped over the side. Elizabeth Gardner turned and walked over to the bucket on the counter. She scooped up a cup of water for Spupaleena and placed it on the pine nightstand beside the bed. Elizabeth knew the young Indian girl would be thirsty when she woke up. She glanced at the girl's hair, wishing she would have washed it a bit more thoroughly. She was able to get the blood and vomit out, but her beautiful hair needed a better scrubbing.

"Phillip, will you fetch me some more wood?" Elizabeth scurried around the cabin collecting supplies to change Spupaleena's dressings.

"Yeah, let me finish fixing this." Phillip sat concentrating on repairing one of his traps.

"I need to make sure I have enough hot water to change these bandages."

"I'll be finished here in a few minutes and I'll get your wood." Phillip continued to fiddle with his trap. A metal piece was bent, and he was having trouble straightening it out.

"Thanks dear, I appreciate your help." Elizabeth whirled around the room making sure each tincture and poultice was concocted just right. "I just want this poor girl to be comfortable and feel safe when she wakes up."

"Uh-huh… she will."

Elizabeth hummed as she gathered her meager medical supplies. She worked in rhythm to the hymns flowing through her mind. It relaxed her hurried behavior.

"Where did you find her?" Elizabeth asked, pouring herself a cup of tea. She walked over and sat in her rocking chair.

"She was on the creek bed, near Twisted Pine Canyon, on the other side of the river. Looks like she rolled down the rocky bluff."

"I can't imagine." Elizabeth shook her head. She sat for several seconds replaying the scene over in her mind. She could not envision tumbling down a hill and the pain that came with it. A shiver ran down her spine. She got up and went to find another sheet to cut more strips.

After placing her clean bandages and a couple of herbal poultices on the kitchen table, Elizabeth shuffled to the stove and stirred her bubbling stew. She put a spoonful in her mouth, licking her lips in approval, and then poured a cup of coffee. Elizabeth breathed

Carmen Peone

deeply, savoring the aroma of venison, onions, and cabbage. She could taste the rich flavor on her lips. She brought the coffee to her husband and sat back down.

"That makes sense. She is so bruised and cut up. I can't imagine what she was doing…or perhaps running from."

"Yeah, I don't know, I couldn't see any sign of animal tracks anywhere." Phillip's eyebrows pulled together as he frowned. "Even if there were, they would be covered up with the fresh snow." He continued to repair his trap.

"I don't think she was hurt before she tumbled down the bluff, but I know she sure did a good job of bang'n herself up during the fall!" Elizabeth motioned to her head.

She took a sip of her husband's coffee and scrunched her nose at the bitterness. Rocking in her chair, she watched the girl, studying her soft features. She admired Spupaleena's high cheek bones and dark skin.

"What a beautiful young girl; her parents must be so worried." She tapped her fingers on her swollen belly. Looking down, she wondered what her baby would look like upon birth.

Elizabeth walked over to the girl. She gently stroked the length of Spupaleena's black tresses and watched the strands run through her fingers. She was reminded of her first baby's dark hair. Elizabeth fought back the tears welling up in her hazel green eyes. She was thankful to be pregnant again. They had lost a son two years earlier and her sorrow was still fresh. Tears rolled down her soft, milky cheeks from time to time, especially when she would uncover his baby clothes while searching for something else.

Elizabeth thought back to the night it all happened. The baby was coming three months too early, and only lived for a few hours. His little lungs were just too weak. He was so tiny, his head fit in the palm of her hand.

Elizabeth prayed she could help Spupaleena, or perhaps help the woman who longed to see her little girl again. Somewhere, there was a mother pacing and wondering if her child was alive. She knew that woman's grief. She understood that woman's tears.

"Phillip, did you get the wood yet?" Elizabeth's voice was faint, but firm.

"I'm almost finished…" Phillip said calmly. "Don't worry, I'll get the wood." He motioned to the door.

Minutes later, Spupaleena began to stir. She opened her eyes and looked around the small cabin, moaning in pain. Her head pounded violently. She felt like she was going to vomit again. She was so dizzy and exhausted, she had to close her eyes and lay still.

"Phillip, I think she's waking up," Elizabeth whispered as she rushed to the bed, feeling Spupaleena's forehead. She tried not to startle the girl in any way, moving fluidly, with the gentleness of a loving grandmother.

Spupaleena moaned as she squirmed in an attempt to find some kind of relief from the pain. Elizabeth quickly soaked a cloth in a bucket of melted snow and placed it on Spupaleena's forehead. She was burning up.

"Phillip, hurry and fetch that wood, we need to keep it warm in here...this poor child," Elizabeth said. "I think pneumonia might be setting in."

Spupaleena's deep moans and jerky movements were enough to get Phillip on his feet and moving. He saw the wrenched look on her face when she made the slightest movement.

"I think she has some bruised ribs by the way she sounds," said Phillip.

"Yeah, I think so." Elizabeth nodded. "We need to gather my cheesecloth. I'll get the Chocolate Tips for her bruising and soreness."

"What else do you need me to get?"

"I need Sumac, Plantain—Rattlesnake not Sagebrush, and the white powder of the Clematis bark; it's in the jar on the shelf above the washtub."

"I see it." Phillip grabbed the needed herbal leaves and powders, setting them in an orderly fashion on the table.

"Oh, I also need the strips I just made for the Sumac and Horsetail that should make a nice poultice." She pointed to the rocking chair where the partially cut sheet lay.

"What else?"

"Nothing, I think that's all. I have water boiling on the stove...oh, heat some more quilts, will ya?"

"Quilts are warming already…" Phillip looked to make sure there were at least two quilts hanging next to the fireplace. The Indian girl's moans caught his attention, bringing his memories back to the previous morning.

When Phillip found Spupaleena buried in several inches of snow, she seemed barely alive. She had her elk robe wrapped around her, which no doubt saved her life. She was cold and her breathing was shallow. Phillip could see that Spupaleena was badly hurt. He had brushed the snow off her, and when he lifted part of the elk robe up, exposing her face and arms, he saw the bruising and gashes. He wished he had known how badly hurt she was and how long she had been lying in the stream bed.

"Thank God there is no water in there this time of year," he mumbled.

Phillip realized that Spupaleena had been out in twenty degree weather, perhaps a day, two at the most. The previous day had been a blizzard that lasted into the late morning. All he knew was the girl needed help as soon as possible. He had tremendous faith in his wife's ability to heal this lifeless child.

"This should be enough," Phillip said. He packed in a load of wood, shutting the door as quickly as he could. A light dusting of snow trailed behind, pushed in by the wind. "What else can I do to help?" Phillip brushed the snow and wood chips off his shirt.

"Well, at this point, we have to let her rest and let God do his work," Elizabeth said. "But for now, you can check on the quilts, don't want them to scorch."

As Phillip re-spread the quilts on top of the chairs, his mind wandered back to when he had found Spupaleena. There was something bothering him; something was wrong. The pressing thought would not let him rest.

He had been confused at what he saw, what looked like a young male snow-covered body, perhaps caught in the storm during a hunt. He saw a corner of elk robe peeking out from under the body. Phillip scooped the snow from the robe with his large hands. He gasped at the sight of a young girl as he uncovered her. A sick and dizzy feeling came over him as he stared at the motionless form.

Phillip leaned down to check the girl's breathing, which was shallow, almost undetectable. Her face was cold and her hair was a mixture of blood and ice. He glanced down, catching the stench of vomit. He wondered how long she had been there. He knew time was short and he needed to work quickly and carefully.

"This is going to be quite the task," Phillip mumbled. He squint his eyes, searching for the best method to lift Spupaleena onto the pole structure he put together with boughs and pelts. He gently lifted the girl on top of the make-shift stretcher, careful to prevent further damage.

Thank God she had her elk robe, he thought. He placed it over her, along with one other blanket, strapped on his snowshoes, and set off. He needed to race and get to the cabin as fast as he could. The young Indian girl needed Elizabeth, who had a special gift of healing. Phillip knew with all of his heart and soul that his wife could save her life.

"Phillip…Phillip." Elizabeth shook his shoulder.

"What? Sorry. I was thinking about yesterday."

"What's wrong? You look like something's wrong. What's bothering you?" Elizabeth rubbed her husband's tense neck and shoulders.

"Something just doesn't add up."

"What do you mean?"

"Well, why would a young girl be out in a blizzard? Isn't that odd to you?" Phillip winced as his wife worked his stiff muscles.

"Yes…"

"I thought she was a he! The covered body looked like what I assumed would be a young man, or teenage boy at least."

"Hopefully, we'll get some answers when she wakes up, assuming we speak the same language." Elizabeth chuckled at the thought. Until now, it had not occurred to her how they would communicate.

That evening, the couple decided Spupaleena was ready for some serious prayer coverage. They had watched the poor girl grimace and groan for several hours, and that, they knew, was enough. Standing over her, the pair tenderly placed their hands on Spupaleena's arms and legs. They prayed over her, asking God for comfort and healing as she tossed and jerked from such intense pain. The longer they prayed the more relaxed and peaceful she became.

Phillip and Elizabeth prayed until she lay peacefully, settling into a calm, rhythmic breathing pattern. They then spread out their own bedding by the fire and crawled in. Phillip drifted off into a restless sleep while Elizabeth remained awake. Her body was exhausted, but her thoughts swirled around in her head like the wind outside their cabin. *This poor girl,* she thought. *What had happened to her? Where was her family? Why was she by herself?* Questions flooded her mind. Elizabeth had to pray herself to sleep in order to finally get some rest.

Chapter 4

Daylight was breaking; the air outside felt calm and crisp. Spupaleena's eyelids fluttered as she struggled to open them. She squinted from the glow of the fire, taking a bit for her eyes to adjust not only from the light, but the pain in her head. Everything hurt. Her arms and legs felt tight and sore. She tried to move, but cringed at the sharpness ripping at her sides. She had never felt this beat-up or weak in her life.

Elizabeth whirled around hearing Spupaleena stir and groan. She hurried to the side of the bed and felt Spupaleena's head. "Still hot," she whispered. She took a cool cloth and caringly placed it over the girl's forehead.

"Good morning!" Elizabeth smiled at Spupaleena. "How are you feeling? Can you understand me?"

"*Kewa* ("Yes")," Spupaleena said barely audible. She knew a lot of English words from her father. He had traded with the white trappers at the Great Falls where they had fished in-tee-tee-<u>huh</u> during the spring and summer runs. He had taught her many English words in order to effectively trade with the white folks.

"Can you try and drink some water?"

"Kewa, I'll try."

Elizabeth dipped a fresh towel in a water bucket and put it up to Spupaleena's mouth. She was able to suck in its coolness. Water had never tasted so pure and refreshing to her, even through a cloth.

"My husband found you two days ago. You're a lucky young girl," Elizabeth said quietly. "I'm sorry but your leg is broken and your head and arms are badly cut." Elizabeth stroked the young girl's hair. "Your ribs are bruised, but I don't think they're broke; you'll heal quickly as long as you rest quietly." She smiled at Spupaleena. Her voice was soft and soothing.

Spupaleena looked at the blonde-haired woman nursing her. She noticed that Elizabeth's eyes were a deep green, so tender and caring. A tear slid down Spupaleena's cheek. She was scared and in so much pain, yet felt completely safe.

"Can you drink some tea? It will help with the pain." Elizabeth dabbed the tears from Spupaleena's cheeks.

Spupaleena gently nodded her head and sucked from a cloth that had been soaked in boiled Yellow Bee plant, making a healing tea.

"My head…it feels like it has been split open…like wood," Spupaleena whispered.

"You took a hard fall. Do you remember anything?"

"Loot." Spupaleena shook her head.

She sucked some more tea from the cloth. She was beginning to relax as the tea eased the pain. Her eyes closed as she drifted off to sleep, soundly this time.

Spupaleena was able to sleep all day and into the evening. She began stirring in the calm of the darkness. The popping of the fire was soothing. The smell of tamarack had always been one of her favorite.

Phillip was tinkering with his traps and Elizabeth was sewing baby clothes in the light of the fire. Dinner had been long over and dishes washed and put away. Elizabeth glanced over at Spupaleena as she began to stir.

"Hello there, how are you feeling tonight?" Elizabeth asked in a chipper tone.

"I feel cha-arre; you say hurt."

"Yes, I bet you do. I want to give you some more tea so you feel better and heal faster." Elizabeth nodded her head. "Is that okay with you?"

"Kewa," Spupaleena said sluggishly.

"I'll make you the tea…it'll help you with the pain and let you sleep soundly."

"Where am I?" Spupaleena asked, while curiously gazing around the room. She had never been in a white man's cabin before. She had only seen the outside on occasion while trapping with her father.

"Well, you're in our home. I'm Elizabeth. My husband, Phillip, found you several miles away, up north and across the river, do you know this area?" Elizabeth said, looking for any indication of recollection.

"Loot, I don't." Spupaleena sighed.

"Get some rest. My husband will be done soon. He can tell you where we are better than I can. He traps in this area, but I don't go with him, so I can't really tell you where he found you."

Spupaleena nodded. Her eyes glistened as she willfully held back tears.

"I'm thirsty, can I have some *see wool<u>th</u>k*, ("Water")?"

"Yes, of course, dear," Elizabeth said. She was tickled to see Spupaleena's desire for something to drink. She hoped the craving for nourishment would come soon. She was too thin as it was. Elizabeth also poured her some healing tea. Grabbing a chair, she sat next to the bed and changed Spupaleena's bandages. She then rubbed salve on her ribs and arms.

"What's your name?"

"Spupaleena," she yawned noisily. The tea was kicking in and her eyelids were growing heavy.

"That's such a pretty name. What does it mean?"

"Rabbit." She took another sip of tea.

Elizabeth moved to her rocking chair. She was amazed at how fluent in English the girl was. She would later have to ask more about her life, knowing Spupaleena was tired and needed as much rest as possible. She picked up the tiny dress she was sewing for her unborn baby. Spupaleena watched her stitch the garment. Elizabeth hummed the sweet sound of "Amazing Grace" while she worked. Her soothing voice helped Spupaleena drift off into a deep, relaxing sleep.

Spupaleena woke up screaming. "*Kunheet, loot...Hooyhuh eklee* ("Help, No, Go Away")." She was soaked with sweat. Her fever had finally broken, but something else poisoned her. Not in her body, but rather something inside, something spiritual. She looked around the room, lit with the morning sun, but no one was in sight.

Suddenly, Spupaleena had never felt more alone. She now remembered all that had taken place concerning her sister. She believed the Creator had come in the night and spoke to her while she slept. She was shaking and her chest felt tight. In her dreams, dark figures chased her. She asked herself if they were trying to chase out her bitterness. Did she need forgiveness? What did she need to do? Confusion wrapped its gnarly fingers around her. She was starving for answers.

She longed for her mother and father. She missed Pekam, but she could never return. She would no longer live a life of beatings. Sadness settled into her heavy heart as a held back tear escaped and slid down her face. She felt like all she had done the last several days was moan and cry. She was sick of her fear and the pain.

Carmen Peone

However, for the first time in her life, she was truly terrified of her future.

As she caught her breath, Spupaleena glanced down at the colorful hand-sewn quilt covering her body. Her eyes fixed on the beautiful colors. It reminded her of her stimteema's quill and grass work. The reds, greens, and blues used to decorate baskets and handbags were like a rainbow. She yearned for her stimteema, but the pain of her past pushed her forward. She could never go back.

Without thinking, she uncovered herself and attempted to sit up. The piercing pain in her head and ribs caught her off guard and slammed her back into her pillow. She groaned and was instantly nauseated. Her throbbing head brought her back to reality. She mumbled a string of native words through clenched teeth. It took several minutes for her to settle down and regain her composure.

She reached down and slid her fingers along the wrapping on her arms. She could feel the splint on her leg, as well as the bandaging around her mid section. She realized she would not be able to go anywhere for weeks, perhaps months. She lay there and let the tears stream down her cheeks. She would have to allow her body to heal. Only then could she search for a different direction, a new start. She would go where her heart led her.

Elizabeth walked into the cabin to find Spupaleena awake. "Oh, hello…" She glanced at the girl and noticed fresh tears. Realizing the young girl would not only need time to heal physically, but also emotionally, she decided to keep to herself for several hours.

"Spupaleena's been through quite a treacherous ordeal—she might not understand the extent of it," Elizabeth said under her breath. She busied herself, quietly tidying up the cabin.

Spupaleena had been raised in a tough world, one where her people had to work hard to stay alive, but she was still so young. She was a child with meager experiences of being out on her own.

"Are you hungry?" Elizabeth asked around dinner time. She walked over to the wood stove and stirred the pot. "I have some vegetable soup warmed up for you...if you think you can eat anything."

Spupaleena just laid there.

"It will be okay," Elizabeth said tenderly, walking to the bed. She prayed and hummed as she sat and stroked Spupaleena's arm.

"Kewa, I'll have some," Spupaleena said after several minutes.

Elizabeth fed Spupaleena and dressed her wounds with fresh bandages. Spupaleena took in some more herbal tea to ease the pain and help her sleep, but the dreams still haunted her. She woke up every morning just before sunrise. She saw herself running away from different things: giant figures, evil looking hawks, and various animals. She needed her tribal healer to set these lingering spirits free. She was beginning to dread sleeping at night for fear of waking in terror.

For the next several days, Spupaleena ate soups and stews, drank her herbal tea, and allowed Elizabeth to care for her wounds. She slept most of the time as her body tried to heal itself. Little by little, the two girls communicated as best they could. Elizabeth attempted to learn new words here and there. Steady progress was made slowly, both verbally and physically. Hope glimmered in the distance.

Chapter 5

Phillip went about his business gathering his pelts and setting new trap lines. The snow was too deep to ride Sammy, his beloved gelding. Even though the middle-aged black-and-white Paint was strong and stout, the three-foot snow drifts would prove too difficult to maneuver.

Every morning, he would strap on his handcrafted snowshoes and walk his trap lines. He would easily snare multiple rabbit, beaver, and muskrat. Once in a while, a martin would find its way on the end of one of the snares.

Phillip trapped all winter, then come spring, would hitch up Sammy to the wagon and head up river with a few other men to the Kettle Falls area to sell his pelts. He also would trade the local Indians for a bit of sun-dried salmon or a basket for his wife. This gave him and Elizabeth plenty of funds to survive the upcoming year.

That's when Phillip had found Spupaleena, during a morning of trapping. He thought he would cross the river, in a communal canoe, and try his luck on the other side of the Columbia River. At daybreak, he strapped on his snowshoes and off he went.

He set a couple of snares here and there along the river. Across the valley, he set a few more at Twisted Pine Canyon. It was midday when the snow began to fall. *One more and then it's time to leave*, Phillip thought. He followed the bend along Rattlesnake Creek, which was dry come late summer and into winter, and stumbled onto the body.

That morning it hit him. She looked familiar. Perhaps they had seen each other one spring at the falls while trading. It was possible. There were so many people there, both white and Indian.

Phillip walked over to the bed Spupaleena was lying on. Yes, something was familiar, but he still failed to place it. In time, things would come together. He had faith that God would put the puzzle together for him. Actually, he knew God already had the answers, he just needed to follow along and let him lead. He learned long ago that God's timing was always perfect.

Spupaleena's head began to heal nicely over the next few weeks and the throbbing slowly disappeared. The following night, however, was not so good. Phillip and Elizabeth prayed over her after she had fallen into a restless sleep. They asked that any harmful spirits leave Spupaleena alone, and asked that the Holy Spirit guide and watch over her, especially at daybreak. She was still having nightmares on a regular basis.

Come morning, Spupaleena awoke crying out. "*Kunheet, kunheet* ("Help, Help")..." Her bedding was soaked with sweat. She was running away from a huge, dark presence. The giant was chasing her through the cold and blackened forest. He wanted her dead. He was about to catch up to her, and then she opened her eyes. But why was he chasing her? What did she do? Spupaleena had a million thoughts and questions running through her head.

She longed for her stimteema's guidance and comfort. *No, I am on my own now,* she thought. A strong independence was showing back up in her life, and she felt the need to make decisions for herself. She could figure this nightmare out. She and the Creator would find the answers. He would walk her through it. He had to. Spupaleena was now more determined than ever.

She began to sing an old song taught to her by her *shahpa* ("Father's Father"). It was a song of healing and protection by the animal spirits that looked after her people. She sang until she believed the evil had gone. She prayed for protection against this giant who haunted her in the night. She would conquer the evil spirit with the help of her Creator. She would pray and sing tonight in preparation for the coming morning. She would be ready.

The following morning proved wrong. Spupaleena woke screaming once again. Her clothes stuck to her sweat-covered flesh. She trembled as the fear curled around her body, reached into her stomach and settled into a knot.

She had the same dream. The same dark forest haunted her. The same ugly giant chased her and the same frightening nightmare grabbed at her intensifying fear. She felt helpless. Her prayers were not working. They were unable to keep her safe. She needed to know what her shahpa would do.

Spupaleena felt betrayed. She asked herself, *Did my ancestors disown me for running away? Didn't they understand that I couldn't remain in my village?* She had to move on. Totally exhausted, she closed her eyes and slept for the rest of the morning. Sometime in the afternoon, when Spupaleena finally woke up, her body felt a bit more rested. Her stomach growled in protest of its emptiness. Dealing with the spirit world was more work than she had ever expected, increasing her appetite. She looked around the room and saw Elizabeth in her rocking chair.

Elizabeth was softly humming a song. *Perhaps a song from her ancestors*, Spupaleena thought. She was hand sewing more clothes for her unborn child.

"*Wi' tuklthmeelwho* ("Hello Woman")," Spupaleena said with a yawn and sleepy eyes.

Elizabeth whipped around in her chair and stared at her, amazed and startled at the same time that the girl was awake and alert. She placed her sewing on the kitchen table and strolled over to the bed. She pulled up a chair and sat down.

"You're much cooler today; your skin has more color to it," Elizabeth said, stroking Spupaleena's forehead. "How'd you sleep last night?"

"Loot, not well," Spupaleena sighed. "I…I have had bad dreams at night…they're starting to scare me…a lot." She hated to admit defeat and confess her fears; so much for figuring things out alone.

"Yes, we hear you in the mornings crying out," Elizabeth said. She took a minute and prayed for wisdom. "What happens in these dreams?" she asked cautiously.

Spupaleena's eyes met Elizabeth's for a moment. She paused to collect her thoughts, looking down at the quilt keeping her warm. She felt Elizabeth might think she was foolish. "I see giant creatures chasing me…the evil spirits that taunt my people, they run after me… they chase me through the forest. I run as fast as I can, but it's never fast enough. It must be because I ran away." Her voice cracked.

She looked away feeling only shame. Spupaleena's eyes came to rest on Elizabeth's swollen belly. That was the first time she actually noticed that the woman was with child. Spupaleena was baffled that she had missed it before.

Elizabeth peered at the girl's dark coal eyes. She could see the fear in them. She could see sadness as well.

Carmen Peone

"Phillip and I hear you toss and turn during the night. We get up and pray over you while you're still asleep. Normally you calm down and are able to rest peacefully." Elizabeth took a sip of water. "Your pain must run deeply, I'm sorry for what you're going through."

"Why…why would you pray for me?" Spupaleena looked puzzled.

"Well, we don't know what you've been through, but we can see that something troubles you. We've found, from our own experience anyway, that God will help us when we ask. We pray so you can find peace. We want to help you heal so you can return to your home. So you can be with your people…with your family."

Spupaleena's brow furrowed and she pursed her lips. The thought of returning home turned her stomach. She would not go back to her home; she could not. She refused to return to her unruly lthkickha. She closed her eyes tightly to avoid the tears that were welling up and threatened to spill out.

"Are you hungry?" Elizabeth asked, changing the subject. She noticed how Spupaleena appeared to shut down. She knew there was some kind of horrific pain, but refrained from prying. She also knew whatever bothered Spupaleena had to be responsible for her nightmares. Elizabeth would have to keep praying for the troubled child. Hopefully, Spupaleena would be more open to sharing her troubles in time. Elizabeth so desperately wanted to help her young Indian friend, who she was becoming deeply fond of with each passing day.

Spupaleena drew in a deep breath and let it out slowly. After a few seconds, she agreed to eat.

During the next several weeks, Spupaleena's appetite increased and her strength gradually began to return. Phillip carved her a walking stick that helped her get up and out of the bed. It was easier to turn around to sit in a chair by the crackling fire, which happened to be her favorite spot in the cabin. This was an improvement that lifted Spupaleena's spirits considerably. She was relieved to sit somewhere other than in bed.

Phillip also built a makeshift bed she could have of her own. Sleeping on the floor made him stiff and sore, not to mention how it made his pregnant wife feel, although she never once complained.

The white man's blankets she welcomed, but never more than her soft and heavy elk robe. The trio began to get into a comfortable routine. There were still minor language barriers, but in time, that to would fade.

Battling the haunting spirits during the early mornings became all too familiar, but they too were diminishing, or so she thought. Spupaleena wondered if the white man's prayers had really worked, or was the Creator forgiving her? She was unsure if he could pardon her without a traditional cleansing ceremony that was normally held during a sweat. She had no idea if she was even worthy of such an immunity.

Carmen Peone

Spupaleena hoped her family could forgive her. She would always love them. At times, when sewing or cooking with Elizabeth, she missed that special time beading or weaving baskets with her toom and stim-teema. Watching Phillip fiddle with his traps made her long for the intimate moments hunting and trapping with her mistum.

Spupaleena thought of how thankful she was that the Creator sent Phillip and brought her to Elizabeth. Spupaleena appreciated the gentle way in which Elizabeth had cared for her. The woman's kindness and nurturing were with such tenderness and compassion. The gradual process of healing taking place in her heart came simply with the love Elizabeth shared with her. She appreciated Phillip's quiet, sturdy manner as well. He was a stronghold that was as solid as the cabin he had built.

Every morning, Phillip walked his trap line; it did not matter if there was three feet of snow or if it was bitter cold, he did his job with a sense of thankfulness. Spupaleena wished she could go and see how the white man captured his prey. She hoped it was not cruel. Her mistum was never cruel. She heard of the white man's jaw like traps that make her animal friends suffer. Her people honored the food that was provided. Suffering was not an option. The pelts were used, but not prized as were some of the white man's.

One afternoon, Spupaleena giggled. "I have a good story to share today." Her face lit up like a full moon on a cloudless night. Elizabeth smiled; she loved to see Spupaleena so excited. Spupaleena enjoyed sharing her native stories with her friend.

"Oh, tell me."

"Okay, this story is about Eagle and Turtle."

Elizabeth put her mending on the table and poured herself and the storyteller a cup of tea. "I'm listening," she said eagerly.

"Eagle was the fastest animal around; no one would race him. One night, a dream came to Turtle telling him that he must race Eagle to set the animal people free."

"That's your people right?"

"Kewa." Spupaleena nodded. "So, Muskrat told Turtle that there was no way he could beat Eagle, but Turtle was set to race him the next day." Spupaleena rubbed her hands together in anticipation. "The next morning, Muskrat took Turtle to Eagle's camp. Eagle said they would race the next day and that if Turtle won, the animal people would be set free. If he won, Turtle would be his." Spupaleena giggled.

"What happened next?" Elizabeth laughed. The tale was a nice change.

"Well, no one, not the animal people nor the other animals thought that Turtle could win. They all laughed at him."

"Aw, poor Turtle."

"Kewa, the next morning, the two met and Eagle asked where they were to race. Turtle announced that he wanted Eagle to pick him up and carry him into the air."

Elizabeth gasped.

"I know!" Spupaleena's face shone with excitement. "So Eagle took Turtle up, he was scared."

"Me too," Elizabeth agreed.

"So Turtle yelled, 'Let go,' and he did." Spupaleena paused.

"What happened next?"

"Turtle dropped fast. Eagle tried to catch him but couldn't. All the animals and animal people watched in amazement. Turtle won!" Spupaleena clapped her hands like a small child.

"Turtle won?"

"Kewa, he won. He claimed himself as chief and let the people go."

"Oh, I love your story," said Elizabeth. "There's always a lesson in your tales. I just love them!"

"Kewa, our stories are meant to teach. We tell them all winter when we're inside. It's nice to share them when baskets are being made and women are beading and sewing."

"Do you like to make baskets and sew?"

"Kewa, but I like to spend time with my mistum the most. Trapping is my favorite. My mistum teaches me a lot. I think he wishes I was a boy!" She laughed.

Story telling was not the only thing that entertained Spupaleena. She was delighted to watch Elizabeth's baby grow inside of her. She giggled at the movements of her swollen belly. It reminded her of Pekam when he was inside her own toom's belly. Spupaleena loved to lay her head on her toom and feel the swirl of his arms and feet against her. The thought of a new life excited Spupaleena. It gave her hope. It reminded her of how new life replaces old ones; lives that are sometimes evil and hurtful.

She hardly cared if Hamis-hamis missed her, or was even alive. She wondered if she could be forgiven for her sour attitude. She was even unsure if she could ever learn to forgive those who had come against her. Anymore, confusion swarmed her quiet times. Spupaleena tried to push such thoughts away from herself, but they eventually came to surface when she was caught off guard.

Chapter 6

It was now well into the winter months. Elizabeth was in her rocking chair reading her Bible. Spupaleena was napping. She was layered in quilts in order to shun the cold. Phillip burst in as the icy air snapped itself through the cabin door. He scrambled inside and hurried over to stand in front of the fire.

"I need to make a trip into Lincoln," Phillip said sharply.

Elizabeth looked up in surprise. "What's the matter?"

"My traps are gone."

"All of them?" She closed her Bible, giving her husband her full attention.

"No, just the ones on the south side of Bitterroot Creek."

Phillip was so angry it never occurred to him that his pants were frozen from falling in the creek. He stood in front of the fireplace shivering, part from the cold and part from rage. In all the time they had settled into the area, nothing like this had ever happened. Respecting other's trap lines was an unspoken law, one of utmost respect; trapping was essential to survival, at lease for Phillip and Elizabeth.

"Phillip, look at your clothes. What happened to you? Are you all right?" Elizabeth rushed over and covered him with a blanket. Phillip looked down in amazement. He just stood there. The commotion startled Spupaleena out of a deep sleep. She stared at the two of them.

"What's happening? Elizabeth, what's wrong?" she asked struggling to sit up.

Elizabeth looked at Spupaleena and then back at Phillip.

"Phillip, why don't you go and change, I'll pour you some hot coffee and then we can discuss the next step," Elizabeth turned to fetch a tin cup. She began humming in an attempt to soothe her nerves. She was stunned with the theft. Her husband worked hard and was an honest man, undeserving of such a crime.

Spupaleena recognized the tune. She had heard it before, but forgot when. She pulled herself out of bed and hobbled to a chair with her walking stick. *Ah, yes, when I first arrived, that same tune*, she thought. Elizabeth's voice had been so soothing. She remembered now. The melody was calming; it made her feel peaceful. She would have to remember to ask Elizabeth about the song later, when things were less tense.

Phillip came back into the room and sat at the kitchen table. He was still baffled. "Why in God's name would someone start stealing now?" Phillip groaned. "It has to be an outsider."

"We don't know, but one thing I do know is we need to pray about it," Elizabeth said. The couple had formed their own family rule in the beginning of their marriage. They decided that no major decision or event, good or bad, would ever be made without prayer. They had also agreed that neither one would ever make an important decision in an extreme emotional state.

After time with the Lord, and nerves settled, it was decided that Phillip would leave in the morning.

"I could go with you—"

"No you won't!" Phillip shot a glance at his wife that would stop a runaway horse.

"Well…"

"Loot!" Spupaleena snapped. Elizabeth and Phillip glanced at each other and then at the girl. Phillip ran his fingers through his hair.

"You're in no condition. Besides, Spupaleena has no business being alone; she's not strong enough," Phillip said, motioning to Spupaleena. She looked back at Phillip, nodding her head in agreement.

"I guess you're right. But I don't want you to go alone. The weather's way too harsh." Elizabeth sat in her rocking chair. She rocked back and forth, sending her husband a look of complete frustration.

"Yeah, okay, I can stop at Hal's place. I'm sure he'll go with me." Phillip chuckled, he was in no mood to argue. His eyes flickered as he looked at Elizabeth.

"Thank you, that'll be good," Elizabeth said with reserve.

Phillip laughed at the overprotection of his wife, his prize. "I would never make it in life without you," he said. Their bond could never be shattered. His love for his wife was too strong. They laughed, breaking the escalating tension.

"Really, can you imagine me traveling in this kind of weather…in this condition?" Elizabeth said, patting her rather large belly. "Even poor Sammy and his sled would struggle to get me on my way."

Laughter filled the room.

Spupaleena looked on in bewilderment as Phillip took a few steps toward his wife, knelt down, and took her into his arms, holding her for a precious moment. Spupaleena was puzzled at their display of affection. Her people rarely carried on in such a manner, at least not in front of each other. She had never felt this tingling inside of her before. She could see the tenderness in Phillip's deep blue eyes when they met his wife's loving ones.

Spupaleena questioned whether or not her parents felt the same way about one another? Spupaleena knew her mistum loved her toom, but looking back, never remembered her parents looking at each other with that kind of love and respect. *How deep was their love?* she thought. Spupaleena wondered if she could ever love that intensely, or be loved in the same manner.

The rest of the day was filled with plans for new trapping supplies and locations. An inventory was made of needed supplies for the cabin. Since he was making the long trek into town, they may as well stock up on a few commodities. Elizabeth went through her storeroom and carefully listed what was needed the most.

Phillip had even sketched a crude map to Lincoln for Spupaleena on the back of a tattered piece of buckskin with charcoal. The map was laid out on the table and Spupaleena was studying it intently.

"When I get back, I'll show you where I found you. We will have plenty of time for that."

"Kewa, I would like that."

"Good." Phillip patted her on the shoulder.

"And you will make me a map of where I fell too?"

"Yes, of course." Phillip smiled, nodding his head toward the map on the table. "I can make you a map of that area too."

Spupaleena was quite appreciative of his support.

"Phillip," Spupaleena said quietly. She became flushed and her heart sped up.

"Yeah, what is it?"

"Are you going to take Sammy with you?" she asked.

Phillip leaned forward and sincerely gazed at her face. He figured she must have held in her curiosity for some time now.

"How do you know about Sammy?" He smiled teasingly.

"I heard you talk about him. I…" she paused, afraid he might be angry with her.

"What is it, Spupaleena?" he asked.

"Can I see him someday—I mean when I feel better and it's okay with you?"

"Why, yes, of course you can. Did you and your family have horses, I mean…do they?" Phillip hesitated, not knowing how to bring up her family, especially because she refused to discuss them. He wanted to avoid upsetting her, but at the same time refrained from skirting around the issue. Sooner or later, she would have to talk about them.

"No, my mistum wouldn't allow it. He said they were for lazy people," she said shyly, not wanting to imply Phillip was lazy.

"Go on." Phillip nodded his head, encouraging her to speak freely.

"There were some families in our village that had them, but my mistum was against it. He also didn't want to feed a *kawup* ("Horse") during the winter. Trapping took too much of his time."

Phillip nodded his head in agreement.

She took a sip of her tea. Looking at Phillip, she saw that he was sincere about her feelings and did not take offense to her lazy comment.

"Do you like horses?"

"Kewa! I have always wanted them. I dream about riding one, running with the wind blowing through my hair, free and…"

Spupaleena was suddenly aware of her excitement and quite embarrassed. She was taught that horses were forbidden and never to be mentioned in the presence of her mistum. Her face felt hot.

"It's okay, you can share your dreams with us. We won't get angry. We love them too. Sammy, he's very special to me. I raised him from a foal and gentled him myself." Phillip grinned, trying to ease her nervousness.

Spupaleena broke out into the biggest smile they had ever seen. For the first time, her eyes danced and sparkled. The couple discovered something their special friend was interested in. They could work with this. Phillip and Elizabeth glanced at each other and laughed. They had not felt this much joy since discovering they were going to have a child. Spupaleena joined in with a girlish giggle. This was a day to rejoice, even in the midst of frustration, God gave them all a glimpse of his favor.

Phillip left at dawn the following morning. It was bitter cold and snowing lightly. Elizabeth was worried, but made a point to place her trust in their Savior. The Lord would give him safe travels. Besides, she could not help but keep the smile on her face from the previous day of laughter. The joy would surely be with her until her beloved returned.

"When will he be back?" Spupaleena asked.

"He should be back in about five days. Travel will just be slow in this weather." Elizabeth nodded reassuringly.

"Will he be safe?"

"Oh yes, my dear. He'll be just fine. I'm sure God'll take care of him," Elizabeth said. She attempted to believe her own words, but continued to feel uneasy. She thought her feelings of anxiousness might be from her pregnancy, but was undecided.

Giving her worries to God was never her strong suit. The whipping wind and heavily falling snow were less than encouraging. Winters could be cruel in that part of the country. Four feet of snow was not uncommon. She knew others had been taken by its cruelty, yet she needed to believe God would provide ample protection to his children.

Chapter 7

Elizabeth tidied up the kitchen after she and Spupaleena finished their breakfast. Elizabeth studied her friend, who was sitting quietly and staring at the fire. She was hoping Spupaleena would open up and share her feelings this week. She looked forward to their time alone. She had prayed fervently that Spupaleena's heart would soften enough to make some kind of connection. She prayed for a deeper conversation, one with meaning and emotion, not just the day's events. Elizabeth believed that a soulful connection could break down the barrier Spupaleena built up around herself. A truth needed to surface in order to release the girl from her nightmares. Elizabeth prayed Spupaleena would be ready.

Elizabeth felt enough trust had been built up in the last several weeks. Now, silence begged to be shattered for deeper healing to take place. Even though Spupaleena's body was stronger, her spirit was drifting away. Elizabeth was thankful for the breakthrough yesterday with Sammy. Hopefully she could somehow use the trusted Paint to bridge the gap.

There was evidence that the Holy Spirit was working. Elizabeth now needed to be patient and trust in God's ideal timing. She had been praying for several weeks for an opportunity to speak with Spupaleena, more importantly to listen. It was a suitable time, with Phillip gone to fetch new trapping supplies. Elizabeth marveled at how God almighty timed his work. How perfect he was. She could envision Spupaleena pouring out her tender little heart, broken and all. It was apparent that God had set up the week for just the two of them. Elizabeth felt she needed to take things slowly and carefully. She, upon waiting for the Lord, would pray, "Father God, please release the stronghold Spupaleena clings so tightly to." Perhaps tomorrow would be the day.

The fog seemed to spill over the mountain tops and surround the tiny cabin. Elizabeth woke up overflowing with cheerfulness and a sense of peace. "Is this the day?" she asked God. She began humming before her feet even touched the floor. She paid no mind to the fog; her thoughts swirled in her head like a warm spring wind.

She slipped into her warmest winter dress and put a pot of water on the stove. She pulled on her coat and strode out the door to care for Sammy. Hopefully this summer they would be able to purchase a second horse so both she and Phillip could ride. Elizabeth loved to ride horses as well. Phillip had even made a special pack to carry the expectant baby in.

"I can't wait!" She took a deep breath, letting the cool, moist air expand her lungs. Her horse would be a palomino. "A nice little mare," she added.

After retuning to the cabin and warming up by the fire, Elizabeth put eggs and bacon on the stove. She puttered around, gathering fabric and picking up around the cabin. She swept the hardwood floor while patiently waiting until Spupaleena rose out of bed. Once she was up and around, they would eat their meal and sit to relax and visit. This was the perfect plan.

"Now that the morning chores are finished, would you like to learn to sew with cloth?" Elizabeth asked eagerly. She had everything ready and held a bundle of fabric out to Spupaleena. "I took the liberty of cutting out a dress for you. We're about the same size, at least when I'm not pregnant." She smiled. "Your buckskin dress is badly torn…"

Elizabeth pointed to the jagged edges worn throughout the buckskin dress. Spupaleena glanced down at herself, then over to the deep green pattern splashed with tiny white and yellow flowers Elizabeth held out to her. She felt the softness of the doeskin, and then allowed her fingers to glide across the white man's thinner fabric. Spupaleena wondered how the light material would keep her as warm.

Elizabeth placed the fabric on her lap. "Spupaleena, I don't want to replace your beautiful dress. I see you worked hard on it and treasure it. We could mend and wash it; in the mean time, you would have a second dress to wear." Elizabeth felt she may have offended her friend.

"My toom and I made it. This was my first dress; I mean the first one I made. I've mended clothing, but never sewed the entire dress before, until this one. My toom helped sew on the fringe," Spupaleena said softly. "But, you're right. I need two dresses, its good." She nodded in agreement.

"We can mend yours up new when you finish this one," Elizabeth said with a sigh of relief. She had tried several times to convince Spupaleena to replace her blood-stained dress, but the girl had always refused.

The pair began working side-by-side. They sewed, talked, and laughed. Everything was lining up just as planned. Elizabeth smiled inside so brightly she felt as if she were glowing.

"At what age do most girls begin to sew?" Elizabeth asked.

"Very young. It's one of the first things we're taught."

"May I ask, then, well…you said this was your first dress," Elizabeth gestured toward Spupaleena.

"Kewa, it is. As a young girl, I've always preferred to trap and fish with my mistum. I suppose I should have been a boy."

The girls laughed. It was good to laugh. Spupaleena was having an exciting morning, hoping to bring up Sammy later that day. She was going to try to talk Elizabeth into walking her out to meet him. She was so thrilled, yet shook inside at the same time. She also hoped Elizabeth would leave her past alone. She was not ready to talk about it.

The dreams still troubled her in the early mornings. She was afraid that discussing her past out loud would cause more harm to come. She was convinced that was how the evil spirits worked. But, she did wonder if it would take place in the white woman's home? Things seemed so different in the cabin. Spupaleena, at times, felt at peace, something she had never before experienced.

"What does your father hunt?"

"Mostly deer and elk," Spupaleena said. She finished sewing a sleeve following every stitch Elizabeth made. She held up her work and smiled. "But he likes trapping small animals the best."

"Pretty good for a metal needle and…let's see…cotton thread?" said Elizabeth. She wrinkled her nose and giggled. "Good work," she added.

"Kewa, I like it."

Elizabeth sat and took it all in. She was proud of Spupaleena's work. Watching her face light up was magical. God was working in this young person. It was as clear as the icicles hanging down from the cabin roof.

"How do you say deer and elk in your language?" She knew the girl loved animals, so that was her starting point.

"Elk is sn'e and deer is stla<u>ch</u>eenum," Spupaleena said slowly and carefully. Elizabeth practiced her new words.

"Could you teach me some more as well?"

"Kewa, I could teach you many words," Spupaleena said, excited to see Elizabeth have an interest in her own culture.

"Good, we could start with the things in the cabin, perhaps tonight after dinner?"

"That'll be fun!" She nodded.

Spupaleena took her completed sleeve and placed it carefully on the table and picked up the other sleeve and began to sew diligently.

"What was it like trapping with your father, you say mistum?" Elizabeth asked. Spupaleena was surprised to hear the word for father in her own tongue.

"Very good! You're a good student," she said smiling. "I would go with my mistum and check our trap lines each morning. We caught many beaver and rabbits. They make good soup; they also keep you warm," Spupaleena said with a girlish smile. She lifted up a foot showing off her rabbit-lined moccasin.

"Very beautiful!" Elizabeth nodded as she slipped her fingers through the gray, velvety fur. "Do your people mostly hunt?"

"Loot, we are the Sinyekst, the Speckled Fish people." Spupaleena said proudly. "Every spring and summer we camp at the big falls up the river from our winter camp site and catch big in-tee-tee-<u>huh</u>, ones that are even bigger than me!" She stretched out her arms.

"That sounds fun. It must be a great amount of salmon to gather. Do you feed just your family?" Elizabeth had so many questions. She was interested in how the Indians lived and raised their families. Even though it was so different from her own upbringing, she was so intrigued.

"No, we all share. We spear or catch them in huge nets. Our men are great fishermen; my mistum, he's strong," Spupaleena sat up a bit taller.

"You must miss him."

"I miss him badly." Spupaleena placed her sewing on her lap. Tears pooled in her eyes, threatening to flow down her soft, tan face.

"Would you like to talk about it?"

Spupaleena shook her head.

"Our men are great fishermen," Spupaleena said, choking on her words.

"I bet they are. You must be proud."

Spupaleena looked away, nodding her head. She refused to let Elizabeth see her cry. Her thoughts drifted to her family. The light in her eyes was blown out with one simple question. Elizabeth's heart sank as she realized she had hit that sensitive spot that remained off limits. "Lord, please heal her heart, her hurts, and take away her fears," Elizabeth prayed under her breath. She was convinced something tragic had happened to her. Perhaps the child was not lost. *But why would she have run away?* she thought. What a foolish thing to do; especially in the dead of winter. The temperature this time of year could prove fatal. Elizabeth's mind took control of itself and she had to rein it in, fast. Assuming was never helpful nor productive. The two sewed in silence for a few minutes.

"If you don't mind, I'm going to take a nap," Spupaleena said as she placed her unfinished sleeve on the table.

"I'm sorry to have upset you…"

Spupaleena said nothing. She simply went to her bed and lay down.

Elizabeth felt terrible. Things were not going so well. She sat and hummed a hymn that had always been special to her, "The Old Rugged Cross." Her mother used to sing this hymn to her as a child. As she hummed, she wondered if the place where Spupaleena's people fished salmon could help reunite Spupaleena to her people.

Perhaps someone knew of this place. Phillip surely had heard of it, or so Elizabeth thought. How wonderful it would be if these falls were the same location he traveled to each spring. She would have to find out more when her husband returned. If it was well known, they could get Spupaleena home to her family.

Chapter 8

The week had passed and Phillip was due home. Elizabeth woke up cheerful. She was anxious for her husband's return. She quickly dressed, stoked the fire, and prepared coffee knowing her husband would be tired and chilled. Spupaleena was still asleep. She had been restless all night. At one point, Elizabeth woke to Spupaleena crying and gasping for air during a dream. She feared that talking about the girl's father stirred up repressed grief. Spupaleena unfortunately, kept her emotions too tightly protected.

Elizabeth sat at the table for her morning quiet time of Scripture and prayer. She was thumbing through the Book of Romans when her gaze locked on Chapter five, verses one and two. "Now that we have been made right with God by putting our trust in him, we have peace with him. By putting our trust in God, he has given us his loving-favor and has received us."

She thought for a moment. Had she been trusting God with Spupaleena or interfering? She was no doubt being tested. She read on. "We are glad for our troubles also. We know that troubles help us learn not to give up." She desperately wanted to know what had happened to hurt that beloved child so profoundly; what were her troubles? "I know, dear God, patience," Elizabeth said quietly, so as not to disturb Spupaleena.

"Please help this child, and bring my husband home safely." She sat in the quiet of the morning, soaking up the Lord's presence.

It had been two days past the expected arrival and Phillip was not yet home. Elizabeth started to pace the room. For once, humming was not soothing whatsoever. He should have been home by now. She rubbed her hands together and pushed her breakfast aside. Pouring a cup of tea, she attempted to fight off her agitation. She sat at the table and picked up her sewing. *I need to calm down, for my baby's sake*, she thought. After making a few stitches, she put the unfinished dress down and stood to peer out the window. No sign of him.

She caught a glance of Sammy down by the barn. Phillip had left enough hay for him to eat for six days. She decided he would need more. Elizabeth grabbed her coat off the peg, slipped into it, adding a stocking cap and gloves, and then headed out in search of hay.

Phillip had always fed; it was his chore, the chore he loved the most.

"This should be easy enough," she said, opening the cabin door.

Elizabeth trudged through the knee-deep snow down to the barn. Sammy nickered at her expressing his hunger. The hay was in the loft. " I should be able to climb this ladder and pitch some down," she said.

"Hello there, boy." Elizabeth smiled. Up she went, chucking down several arm loads of hay. Wiping her gloves and coat off, she then climbed back down the ladder. It had been easier for her to get up the steps than to come down with her protruding belly. Before heading back to the cabin, she paused to give the gelding a treat. She rubbed his fluffy, thick winter coat and off she went.

Spupaleena was now awake and sitting up at the edge of the bed. "I wondered where you were," she said.

"Good morning. I happened to look out the window and see Sammy. He looked hungry." She stood by the fire for a moment soaking in the warmth. "I know Phillip left food for several days, but I wasn't sure if he was out or not." Elizabeth shed her winter coat, hanging it up by the door. She tossed her mittens and hat in a box underneath the coats.

"And?" Spupaleena always lit up when there was talk of Sammy.

"Well, he was out, so I found some and now he's happy!"

Elizabeth gave a nervous laugh. She felt like a child who was suddenly caught with her hand in the cookie jar.

"Where did you find the hay?" Spupaleena asked.

"It was in the loft—"

"You did not climb up there and get it!" Spupaleena interrupted.

"Yes, I did. Phillip has a sturdy ladder built right into the loft; they're attached." Elizabeth said in her best matter-of-fact voice. "Certainly, you can't go. Besides, I'm just fine, see?" She twirled around in a silly fashion.

"Kewa, you are just fine," Spupaleena echoed sarcastically.

"Did you pet him? How is he? Is he warm enough?" she asked eagerly.

"Yes, he's doing very well." Elizabeth walked to the bed and fetched her sewing basket out from underneath.

"I'm glad he's warm; it has to be cold out! I felt the breeze when you opened the door."

"Yes, it's a cold day today. But all is fine." Elizabeth turned to fetch some steaming tea.

"Give him an extra rub for me next time!" Spupaleena smiled and her eyes sparkled with excitement.

"Okay, I will, just for you." Elizabeth winked. "Soon enough, you will be able to do it yourself."

"Oh, I hope so. I can't wait! He is so *sweenoopt*, ("Handsome")." Spupaleena's face glowed in the fire, she was so excited. She badly missed her animal friends back home.

Elizabeth poured their tea and brought it to the table. She sat in silence as Spupaleena washed up and changed into her day dress. Spupaleena's heart was softening and she was talking more, but the words were merely brushing the surface. Actually, that was alright with Elizabeth. Her mind was heavy on Phillip today. Although the skies were clear, the air was frigid. He should be able to return today for sure. She was trying to be strong and trusting.

"Are you feeling well?" Spupaleena asked.

"Um…yes. I'm worried about Phillip."

"Me too. But he's a strong man, right?" She smiled, attempting to comfort Elizabeth. "He should come home soon."

"Yeah, he is strong and we just have to trust God to get him home unharmed. Would you be willing to pray with me?"

"Kewa, I will, if you think your God will listen." Spupaleena looked confused.

"Oh, my sweet girl, yes, he will listen!"

The two prayed together for the first time. Elizabeth was delighted. Phillip will surely come home soon with the two of them praying. Elizabeth felt a renewed peace and comfort. "No matter what, God is always in control," she reminded herself.

Three days later, Phillip had not yet returned. Not only was Elizabeth's faith being tested, but the baby would be coming soon. She teetered the fine line between worry and outright panic. She knew God always answered prayer, but this time, she sensed, it may not be the way she desired.

She needed Phillip. She needed him to be there for the birth of their baby. She needed him just to be her husband, her comforter, and protector. She hated being confined in the cabin with nothing to do but fret. She paced and hummed and paced some more.

"Elizabeth, sit down. Should we pray again to your God; could we not have prayed hard enough?"

Elizabeth stopped. She turned to Spupaleena slowly and thoughtfully. "Spupaleena, my dear child, God always hears our prayers. It's not a matter of praying enough; it's a matter of waiting patiently for his response …and as you can see, I'm having trouble in that area." Spupaleena smiled at the woman who always had an answer.

"What should we do?" Spupaleena asked eagerly.

"Well, there isn't much we can do. Neither of us is in any condition to venture out. Besides, there's too much snow on the ground and it's too far to walk. We'll just have to trust and wait."

"But, I'm healing—"

"No, you are not healed enough."

Carmen Peone

"Kewa, I come from a people that are strong and I can make it at least to Phillip's friend's cabin. I can see if they are there." Spupaleena squared her jaw, standing tall and confident.

Elizabeth took in a deep breath and let it out slowly, rubbing the back of her neck. She looked at the girl with great respect.

"Spupaleena, I know you are strong in your heart, as are your people. But, you are in no condition to travel. Your leg is not yet strong enough, nor your ribs." Elizabeth spoke gently, trying to make her point. "They take many months to heal—"

"But," Spupaleena interrupted.

"No! You are not ready. You will only hurt yourself more; your body will not heal if you go out now. We'll wait," Elizabeth said softly. "The weather is just too cold and the snow is too deep. We'll be just fine, and God willing, so will Phillip."

Elizabeth rose up from her chair, and poured herself and Spupaleena a fresh cup of tea. "Now, let's finish your new dress." She motioned to the sewing basket. "It's coming along nicely. Maybe you could teach me some more words. What is the name of your people again?"

Spupaleena looked at her friend, shrugged her shoulders, and sat down.

"Please, tell me more about your way of life." She gave her friend an assuring smile. "I enjoy learning from you; let's focus on something other than fretting about my husband, or we will both likely go crazy."

Spupaleena gave up in defeat. She realized no one could win an argument with Elizabeth. The woman was a rock that could not be budged. She was a woman of faith and strength, sprinkled with a dash of headstrong.

"Like I said before, we are of the Sinyekst, the Speckled Fish people. We are a people who walk with the water—whisthuh eel e seewoolthk. We walk the streams and river fishing for in-tee-tee-huh and other fish," Spupaleena said, trying not to show her frustration.

She was delighted to share her language and culture with Elizabeth, she was happy to teach, it made her feel important and appreciated, something her lthkickha never made her feel since their mother's death. But she still pouted because Elizabeth had shot down her idea of going to the neighbors. She was going stir crazy in the cabin. Fresh air would have been welcoming.

"Do you sing much in your family?" asked Elizabeth.

"Kewa, my toom and I sang all the time."

"Would you sing for me?"

Spupaleena put her hands in her lap and thought for a moment.

"I can sing a song for you, for Phillip." Spupaleena nodded. "It's a song we sing often for our men to come home safely from a hunt."

"That sounds good." Elizabeth struggled to hold back the tears as Spupaleena began her song. She was touched by her affection. Spupaleena closed her eyes and held up the palm of her hands to the Creator. She sang with a depth in her heart never displayed before. Her voice echoed in the tiny home and settled in their hearts. The song brought comfort to them both.

Elizabeth sat with her sewing in her lap and just listened. She closed her eyes and pictured Phillip. He was home and safe. He had purchased his trapping supplies and was in the cabin and had them all lain out on the table to show the girls. She pictured him laughing and joking. His eyes dancing as he told stories from his trip. She saw him warming his hands by the popping fire while she sat in her rocker; Spupaleena sitting on her bed listening intently. She saw it all so vividly. She smelled the smoke from the fire on his shirt. She smelled the horse hair on his sleeves and hands after he had rubbed Sammy before coming into the cabin, no doubt giving him a special treat first.

Surely he would be home soon. "Please God," she prayed.

Chapter 9

It was late in the afternoon, but the sun lifted everyone's spirits. Elizabeth and Spupaleena were diligently sewing—keeping busy really. The baby would come sometime soon. Elizabeth could tell that her belly had dropped.

There was no wind, so they heard the crunchy footsteps nearing the cabin. Both girls looked up and glanced at each other. Elizabeth tossed her sewing on the table and scrambled for the door. She opened it, only to see a stranger coming her way.

"Ma'am, you Elizabeth Gardner?" asked the old mountain tracker.

"Yes, yes I am," she replied, a bit startled.

"May I come in? I…I have some news for ya ma'am," he said, shifting his weight from side-to-side.

"Yes, of course," Elizabeth held the door open. "Please sit down, would you like some coffee to warm up with?"

"Please." He drew in a deep breath and blew it out nervously.

Elizabeth knew something was wrong with Phillip, but how bad? Her heart pounded. She could barely pour the rugged-looking man some coffee without spilling it.

"Now, mister…"

"My name's Bunker, ma'am," he said, taking his hat off and setting it on his lap. His manners were surprisingly pleasant considering how rough he looked.

"Mr. Bunker, you have some news?" Elizabeth wrung her hands while her heart felt like it would beat right out of her chest.

He looked at the Indian girl with curious eyes. Spupaleena looked down and her face turned red. "Please excuse me, this is my friend Spupaleena, now Mr. Bunker, your news," Elizabeth persisted.

"Ma'am, is your husband…his name Phillip Gardner?"

"Yes, it is. Have you seen him, is he all right?"

"Well ma'am, I…well I…" Bunker wiped the sweat from his brow. From his pained expression, Elizabeth knew things were looking grim.

"What is it? What's happened?" Elizabeth urged, using all her energy to remain calm.

"Ma'am, there was an accident, your husband was head'n home, an…well, he wuz jumped by a couple of thugs. He wuz beat up perdy good when I found 'em. He wuz able to tell me your name and 'bout where ya live. Ma'am, he will live, but…" Bunker hesitated.

Elizabeth just sat there. She wrapped her arms around herself trying to stop from trembling. She was dizzy, willing herself not to throw up. She could hardly believe what she was hearing.

"There must be some mistake. He can't…" Elizabeth drew in a sharp breath.

"Ma'am, I'm sorry, it was your husband, Phillip Gardner."

"But, well, where…" She swallowed around the lump pushing against her throat. "Men beat 'em up?" Tears poured down her cheeks.

"Yeah, they seemed to be look'n fer money or somethun. They had them a knife…and…well, cut 'em up good—"

"How bad?" Elizabeth cupped her hands over her mouth.

"Perdy bad, ma'am. Sorry to have to bring ya the news. I don't…" Bunker was at a loss for words. He took a sip of coffee.

"I wasn't able to bring 'em back, his leg's perdy mangled, ma'am. I figured I'd spare ya the sight; he's with the doc in Lincoln…may lose his leg." Bunker looked down at the wooden floor and just held his hat in his lap. He noticed the sweat trickle down the side of his face and wiped it off. A sideways glace revealed that the woman was with child. Bunker swallowed hard.

Elizabeth sat, staring at the man. Spupaleena was not sure what to say or do.

"Um, there was a man with your husband."

"Yes, Hal, is he all right?"

"No, ma'am, I'm sorry. He didn't make it."

"No, God, please no!" She cupped her head in her hands and broke down.

Spupaleena stood behind her and held her tight, speaking softly. After a few minutes, Elizabeth got herself together, but was in shock and needed to lie down.

"Ma'am, is there anything I can do to help ya out 'fore I leave. I have to be gitt'n here 'n a bit," Bunker said. He was not sure what to do. The three sat in silence.

Elizabeth looked at him with her soft, sad eyes. "Will you take me to him?"

"Ma'am, you're hardly—"

"Hardly! What?" she snapped. "I'm just fine; this baby isn't to come for a few days." She stood and walked to the fire place.

Spupaleena hobbled over to Elizabeth and grabbed her by the shoulders.

"Loot! You're upset." Spupaleena lowered the tone of her voice. "Maybe the man will go give a message to the doctor… someone will bring him back. Kewa, the man can get the family that lives up the valley." She glanced at Bunker, nodding her head in that direction.

Elizabeth wiped her brow with her sleeve. Her knees felt like they would buckle underneath her. She leaned against the hearth groaning. Spupaleena held on to her, but the girl could no longer hold Elizabeth's weight. Bunker jumped to his feet and caught Elizabeth as she sank into his arms. She covered her mouth with the palm of her shaking hand, unable to stop herself from sobbing uncontrollably, partly due to relief that her husband was alive, but also in mourning for his health and safety. *How does a trapper trap with only one leg? It's his passion*, she thought. Bunker laid the woman in bed and headed outside, tears rolling down his stern face.

Bunker had to do something. He knew Phillip's missus could have her child any time and he could not just leave her stranded. He picked up an axe and started chopping wood. He could at least make sure the two girls would be warm for the next several weeks. The girl was injured and hardly any help.

He noticed Sammy in the corral. He walked over to assess the situation. He could see the horse was low on hay. Bunker climbed up the ladder and threw down enough hay for a number of days, which would get him by, at least for now. He looked around and noticed that a slow-flowing stream ran through. The gelding could surely break the ice to get a drink.

Elizabeth seemed to calm herself down. She stood to get a glass of water, although a bit light-headed. Her eyes were swollen and she was still slightly quivering.

Her sadness instantly turned to anger. Why had God allowed Phillip to be attacked by such cowards? The baby was coming any day now. A child they had prayed so fervently for. "Why?" she asked. Suddenly, a different pain showed its face. Elizabeth doubled over.

"Elizabeth, what is it?" Spupaleena shrieked.

"I think it's time—the baby's coming," Elizabeth moaned.

"What do I do? I have never done this before." Spupaleena frantically scanned the room, what for she was unsure. "What do I need to get?"

This was about all the excitement the girl could handle. Outdoor life she knew: how to trap animals and pick the correct herbs, but not to deliver a baby. Spupaleena knew nothing. Her sister had always been the one to assist in these kinds of situations.

"It's all right, Spupaleena, calm down." Elizabeth wiped her brow with her apron. "It'll be all right. I've had plenty of experience with birthing babies in my day. I'm the oldest of ten brothers and sisters, not to mention assisting with various other relations when giving birth." A pained chuckle escaped her.

"What do I do first?" Spupaleena asked as she began to calm down. She took in a couple deep breaths.

"Well, first find Bunker, we will need plenty of wood in here for the night. The baby will have to be kept warm, and then find an old sheet and tear it in half. We'll use that to wrap the baby in…" Elizabeth breathed through a contraction, leaning on the bed for support. She cried out, remembering the pain she had with her first baby.

Bunker heard the scream, dropped the axe, and headed for the door. He nearly ran Spupaleena over as she cracked the door open, calling out for him to gather wood and bring it in. He nodded and started gathering an arm load he had just split.

"What am I supposed to do…a baby!" Bunker trembled all over, completely unaware of Spupaleena staring at him in disbelief.

"God, if you exist, help," he prayed, now breathing heavily.

Back inside, Spupaleena gathered the sheet, towels, a basin, and pitcher of water.

"What now?" she asked, setting the supplies on the table. She glanced at Elizabeth. "I'll get you a cool cloth to wipe your face with."

The creaky door opened. "Here's the wood ma'am… oh, um…is…" Bunker shut the door and stood wide-eyed, frozen in his steps, sickly aware of what was happening. His face was flush, looking around for a place to drop the wood before he passed out.

Carmen Peone

"Just drop it over by the stove, Mr. Bunker, and come help me get into bed. Spupaleena can't put that much weight on her leg and her ribs are bruised," Elizabeth said through gritted teeth as another contraction came over her.

Bunker did what he was told. "If there's nothing else, I think I'll just take myself back outside and fix ya up some more wood." Dark was soon approaching. He searched for a lantern and match then darted outside.

"Yes, that would be good." Elizabeth nodded, wondering how Phillip would be acting at this moment. She wished he were there to welcome their new baby into their arms, not just hers. She missed him like never before.

Spupaleena finished getting things ready just as Elizabeth instructed her. She hurried over to Elizabeth with a fresh cloth and wiped her face and back of her neck.

Another contraction came and Elizabeth screamed. Bunker could hear her from outside and he just kept on chopping wood. He had never been in a situation like this before and vowed to never put himself in it ever again.

Spupaleena held Elizabeth's hand, continually patting her with the cool cloth. She sang lullabies in her native tongue, hoping to soothe her friend.

A couple of hours later, a baby girl was born. She was pink and healthy.

"My friend, you did a fine job," Elizabeth said. She was exhausted and happy that this baby came quicker than her first. She was elated and torn at the same time. She desperately wanted to share this precious moment with her husband.

"You did the work," Spupaleena laughed. "I'm sorry Phillip isn't here to be with you." She took the baby's tiny fingers in her own.

"Me too. He'd be so proud." Elizabeth's tears shone through her beaming smile as she gazed at her newborn daughter.

Spupaleena kept an eye on the baby so her exhausted mother could get some rest. She was wide awake anyhow. The excitement of being a part of the birth was exhilarating.

She, for the first time, saw the miracle of birth, knowing only God could provide such a wondrous event.

"Kewa, *lim lumt* ("Thank You"), Creator, for this gift from you," she whispered. This was the beginning of believing that Phillip and Elizabeth's God was indeed real. The birth of a baby, she decided, was nothing short of a miracle, and only something God could give.

She sat and stared at the tiny bundle in her lap. She rocked back and forth, aware of a feeling never before felt, a love and joy she never knew before that day. She loved Pekam, her baby brother, but was absent when he was born. She discovered a special kind of love after witnessing the birth of a baby.

Bunker stayed on through the night. He waited until he could hear movement in the cabin and then cooked a meager breakfast for the three of them. He made sure the ladies had all they needed before he said his good-byes.

Elizabeth understood that he needed to move on. She knew his type, a drifter. The two women would make it. They had food, heat, and the Lord. Even though Elizabeth questioned why God allowed Phillip to be attacked, she would trust him—in the good and difficult times.

Spupaleena cared for the baby and Elizabeth for the next several days until Elizabeth was up and ready to resume some of her daily chores. She knew the chores would help strengthen her body, eventually.

"I wish I could help better. I feel so...so weak," Spupaleena said.

"I think the word you're looking for is useless and you're far from that! You're still healing, Spupaleena. You'll heal in time." Elizabeth rocked her baby girl, stroking her tiny pale face and bald head. "I'm fine and so is baby. With you helping us, we're in good hands." She grinned. "We'll make it."

Spupaleena did feel good returning the favor; she was delighted, tending to Elizabeth for a change. She watched the pair for a few minutes. "Have you decided on a name yet?"

"Yes, I have. I think I'll call her Hannah Marie Gardner. What do you think?" Elizabeth searched Spupaleena's face for her reaction.

She paused to consider the name. "Kewa, Hannah Marie, that's a good name," Spupaleena smiled down at the babe in her mother's arms.

"Marie was one of my sister's names. She was one of the little ones who died. She was only five." Elizabeth clutched her daughter near her heart. She closed her eyes and rubbed the baby's back. The stillness was calming. The crackling of the fire relaxed Elizabeth, allowing her to enjoy her newborn, not yearning for Phillip as much.

"What happened? Was she sick or hurt?"

"She died of pneumonia." Elizabeth kissed Hannah, taking in the sweet baby aroma.

"She was tiny and fragile, sick all the time."

"I'm sorry. We had a young one in our village that also died as a little girl. It was sad and happened not too long ago."

"Did you love her?"

"Yes, very much. She was beautiful. My mother loved her too."

Spupaleena considered what it would have been like to have a sister to laugh and play with. She grimaced at the thought of ever enjoying time with her sister, let alone loving her. Not a single memory of them having a fun adventure together came to mind. It made her shiver.

Elizabeth retired to bed, sad, exhausted, and lonely. She wanted time to herself, to think and pray. She asked God for wisdom and discernment. She wanted to be a confident example for Supualeena, for her to see and be able to feel the Lord's strength and comfort. A woman who cried all the time and took pity in herself only proved to be vulnerable.

It was late in the morning. Elizabeth had had time in her devotions. She dressed for the day, and without thinking, walked to her coat.

"What are you doing?" Spupaleena said.

"Huh?" Elizabeth turned to her with a blank look in her eyes. "I'm going to get some wood for the fire."

"Loot!" Spupaleena took the coat away from her friend and escorted her to the table. "I have already done that and now breakfast is ready."

Elizabeth sat in a daze, not quite awake. "I guess I really don't have much energy yet." She rubbed her eyes.

"There's enough wood in the pile until tonight." Spupaleena brought Elizabeth a plate of fried eggs and hotcakes. "I'll get more later." Bunker had chopped smaller pieces that the girls could easily handle.

Elizabeth looked down at her plate. "You made hot-cakes?"

"Kewa, don't looked so shocked, I've been watching you for a long time now." She passed her the syrup. "I'm a quick learner."

Elizabeth took a bite, not sure what to expect.

"Mm, this is delicious." She was so hungry she gobbled down every morsel.

After breakfast was finished and the rest of the chores were done, the girls just sat around and enjoyed Hannah for the remainder of the day. Everything else could wait.

The air felt fresh and crisp on Elizabeth's face. She was happy to be outdoors, if only for a few minutes. She finally felt at peace now that she had aired her feelings to God. She knew he listened. She knew he loved her. She also knew she needed to trust him wholly. God was leading her down a path and only he knew the way. What she needed to do was follow and trust.

Elizabeth figured it was now time to decide the best way to connect with her husband. It had been six days since Bunker left. He agreed to get a message to her nearest neighbors. They were a half day's ride, so on foot in the middle of winter, it would take much longer. She took in a deep, cleansing breath and went back inside.

Elizabeth walked over to the fire and tossed a couple of logs on the brilliantly, glowing coals. She went to her chair and slowly sat down. She had no real expression on her face. She was simply deep in thought. Spupaleena managed to hobble over to the table gripping a cup of steaming tea for the new mamma. Baby Hannah was fast asleep in Bunker's makeshift cradle.

The night Elizabeth gave birth, Bunker sat out back not really knowing what to do. He had never walked into a situation quite like the one he then faced. He had scanned the rubble left out back, he presumed, left by Phillip. There were pieces of wood everywhere, some were scraps scattered about, and other pieces were neatly and precisely chiseled. The longer Bunker stared at the rubble, the more he recognized the beginning of a baby cradle. It seemed to him that Phillip began cutting out the sides of the cradle made of pine. Phillip had just gotten started. There had been plenty of time to finish the project, so it seemed. Bunker scratched his head.

"How long has 'e bin gone?" he said shaking his head.

Bunker had scrounged around locating nails and an old rusty hammer. He decided to throw together a bed for the woman's baby. He felt bad for her, a husband who was in a bad way, and a baby about to come into the world. The newborn would need something to sleep in. Looking around, he noticed a broken handsaw half buried in the snow. *Was that why Phillip had gone to town?* He thought. No one traveled in the winter unless it was absolutely necessary.

Phillip, knowing his baby would be coming, perhaps trekked through the snow and wind so the child could sleep in a fancy, warm bed. Bunker shook his head again. He did not understand such nonsense. To journey that far for a saw was absurd. There must have been another reason. Who in their right mind would leave his young, pregnant wife and a young, injured girl behind to fend for themselves.

Bunker shook his head. "I guess it's none of my business," Bunker mumbled. He would never know.

He finished the shabby cradle the best he could with the tools he had. He felt good when the cradle was complete. He felt worthy for the first time in several years. That morning, when the ladies were still asleep, he proudly carried the cradle inside, stoked the fire, and sat at the table until Elizabeth awoke.

"What is this?" Elizabeth said, startling Bunker, who was staring into the smoldering flames.

"Ma'am, you're awake. Uh, it's a bed…for the baby… do ya…well, ma'am, do ya like it?" Bunker was nervous, not sure the woman would want the wooden, uneven box of a bed sitting at his feet. He never was good with wood, only hunting and skinning.

"Like it?" Elizabeth jumped up and strode over to the new bed for her precious little one. She let her fingers glide over the sweet smelling pine. "I love it! How…where…"

"I saw the pieces out back and figured your mister was fix'n it for your new one." Bunker was a bit flustered. He was not used to people making a big deal over him. His face felt hot and his hands were sweaty. "I hope ya don't mind—"

"Mind? Heavens no, Mr. Bunker. Thank you so much. It's perfect," Elizabeth said. She felt so blessed to have this stranger care so much to go out of his way and provide for their needs. "Thank you very much. May God bless you and your travels."

"Thank ya, ma'am. I hope your husband'll…he'll come home soon." He stood for a moment looking into Elizabeth's deep green eyes with compassion, turned, and walked out the door.

Chapter 10

Elizabeth sat in silence, admiring Hannah as she lay asleep in her cradle. A yellow and green floral quilt Elizabeth had sewn for her first child covered the baby. Hannah looked so peaceful and innocent. Her skin was creamy and her head scarce with golden, down-like hair, a true gift from the Lord above. As Elizabeth gazed at her daughter she let her thoughts flow freely through her mind. She felt so relaxed and unguarded. She was glad Spupaleena had been around to see the power in the miracle of birth.

Her eyes were fixed on her darling bundle, and she was deep in thought. After a while, her mind grew restless and a speck of plotting crept its way in. Elizabeth was a master at planning and sorting out problems. Shaping resolve, as a potter molds his clay, was one of her gifts, or so she thought.

Carmen Peone

Spupaleena needed to see Elizabeth's absolute reliance on the Lord; her plans would have to align accordingly. She could already see where she had failed miserably. It was a tall order God asked of her. But he always used ordinary people for his service. She just needed to remain willing. *All of the apostles were ordinary*, she thought.

Elizabeth had such mixed emotions stirring around inside of her, excitement was the strongest. She would have to take things moment-by-moment, prayer-by-prayer.

Jack Dalley, the Gardner's neighbor, had finally trudged in to Lincoln and saw Phillip. They had made small talk, as Jack could see his friend was in bad shape. The doctor told him that Phillip would need to stay put for a month or more. They talked for some time; he wanted to get as much information about Phillip for Elizabeth as he could. He wanted to leave nothing to question. The doctor had shared with Jack the details of the accident and the condition he was in.

Phillip had not, however, been told that his baby daughter had been born. Bunker, for whatever reason, had withheld the news of the birth. The only information offered was that, "All was well at the cabin."

The amputation of Phillip's lower leg left him with fire-like pain running up and down the stump throughout the days. The doctor called it phantom pains and kept him heavily medicated to dull the pain as best he could. Perhaps that was a blessing. He desperately needed to see his wife, especially knowing she could have their baby any day now.

He beat himself up, knowing he should be there with her. What a failure he was. What kind of a husband leaves his pregnant wife? "Oh God, forgive me," he begged.

Jack picked up some supplies for Elizabeth and headed back to the Gardner's cabin. The air was frigid, but the sun shone and the brightness lifted Jack's spirits. He was also a believer and knew God would heal his friend, reuniting the couple in time.

A few days later, Jack reached the cabin. He told Elizabeth all he knew and reassured her that Phillip would heal and return as soon as he could travel. But the biggest shock came when he saw the baby. "If only I had known," he said.

"No, it's okay," Elizabeth said in a gentle voice. "Phillip will know about his daughter when the time is right. He has enough to deal with right now. I just want him healthy and home."

Jack chopped more wood for the ladies, cared for Sammy, promised to help bring Phillip home when the time came and went on his way.

The air outside began warming up and winter was coming to an end. It was still a bit chilly in the morning, but the snow was quickly melting. The girls were adjusting to Hannah's schedule, and she was nearly sleeping through the night, at least until daybreak.

Spupaleena was gathering a few pieces of firewood, as best she could with a limp and a walking stick. She stole a moment to take in the beauty of the sunrise. The gelding nickered and caught her attention. She stood and smiled, dreaming of riding him around the corral. "Someday soon, Sammy," she promised. She brought an armload of wood in and stoked the fire. She stood momentarily, gathering up her courage. "I would like to go see Sammy," Spupaleena caught herself holding her breath and blew it out. Elizabeth looked up, she was reading out of Psalms, her favorite book in the Bible.

"Well now, what do you have in mind?"

"I want…I just want to feel his mane and rub my fingers through his fur."

"Yes, we could do that, but I must tell you, he has hair, not fur." They both laughed. Spupaleena's face reddened.

"The afternoons are warmer, so we can go then." Elizabeth nodded her head with a big grin.

"I need to knit Hannah a warm hat so she can venture out with us. What color should I use?"

Spupaleena shrugged her shoulders. "I don't know," she said, grinning. She was so excited to finally get to touch the gelding. Her mind raced with questions; what would he feel like? What would he smell like? She had never been close to a horse before. But some days she could smell the most wonderful scent after Phillip had been with him.

"Will you go over by the end of the bed and get out my yarn from the trunk? Let's have a look. Hannah is almost done feeding." Spupaleena hobbled over to the end of the bed. As she searched through the skeins of yarn, she picked up a sweater she discovered in the trunk.

She held it up to Elizabeth. "This is nice and warm."

Elizabeth glanced over and froze. She sucked in a breath as her foot came up and kicked the turned-over crate her tea was resting on. Her cup tipped over, shattering on the wood floor, splashing tea everywhere.

"That's Phillip's sweater, I made it for him when we were first married. Where did you find it?"

"It was in the bottom of all your yarn."

Elizabeth placed the baby in her cradle, hurried over, and grabbed the sweater right out of Spupaleena's grip. She put her face in it and took in a deep breath, hoping to get a whiff of Phillip's scent. She let it out and tears streamed down her face.

"I miss him so much!" she cried.

Spupaleena didn't know what to say. She stood and wrapped her arms around her friend and held on. She let Elizabeth cry, but not alone. She could not hold back her own hot tears, as she also missed Phillip.

Elizabeth had forgotten about the sweater, until now. After she gained a little self-control, Spupaleena released her. She stroked the softness of Phillip's sweater. Elizabeth thought that a creamish colored yarn enhanced Phillip's sapphire eyes, but he thought it was too feminine, so he only wore it a couple of times. He had hidden it under the yarn hoping she would forget about it, at least for a while. The last thing he wanted to do was hurt Elizabeth's feelings and announce that he outright despised the girly colors.

"Are you all right?" Spupaleena watched Elizabeth.

"Yes, yes, I'm fine. I wish he was here with us." Elizabeth got up and sat in her chair, rocking gently in a soothing motion. "I feel so empty without him. I want him to see his baby girl."

"I miss him too," Spupaleena admitted. She hobbled over and plopped herself down at the table. The rest of the morning, the girls were quiet. Elizabeth read her Bible and prayed in between caring for Hannah. She faked a strong impression, but inside felt like a total wreck. She was blind in that her own humanness was Spupaleena's greatest inspiration.

Sometime the following afternoon, Elizabeth decided it was time to introduce her friend to Sammy. They were tired of being cooped up in the cabin. Stretching their legs and breathing in some fresh air would be invigorating.

"I think it's time to go for a walk," Elizabeth announced, winking at Spupaleena.

She looked up with her big, coal eyes. "What? Oh, we get to go see Sammy?" Spupaleena tossed her quilt aside. "Kewa, I'm ready." Spupaleena hopped out of bed, overwhelmed with excitement.

"I'll bundle up Hannah, and then we'll be ready. I can't wait to see how she looks in her new hat!"

Spupaleena scrambled to the door as fast as her gimp leg would take her. She grabbed her coat off the hook, trembling with anticipation.

Once in the corral, Spupaleena ran her fingers through the gelding's velvety, winter coat. She stroked his neck and withers. Taking his mane in her hands, she gently buried her face in them and took a deep, gratifying breath. She rubbed his mane on her cheeks, closing her eyes and absorbed the moment. A dream at last transformed into a reality.

"I have waited all my life to touch you, to smell you, my friend," Spupaleena said, speaking softly to him. She

Carmen Peone

leaned into the horse and stroked his muzzle, allowing her fingers to run down the length of his nose.

Elizabeth quietly watched, feeling she had taken the animal for granted. She merely stood, cuddling Hannah, witnessing a wish come true.

Spupaleena enjoyed one last waft of horse smell. Rubbing Sammy's eyes in both her hands, she whispered, "You are as wonderful as I had hoped you could ever be."

A scream pierced the still morning. Spupaleena's nightmares were back. Beads of sweat saturated Spupaleena's forehead and streamed down the sides of her face. Her body trembled as if something had possessed her.

"Spupaleena! What's the matter?" Elizabeth rushed to her side and shook her, trying to wake her up.

"Loot! Loot!" Spupaleena yelled, terrified.

"Spupaleena, what's the matter…talk to me. Who are you saying no to?"

"They're back…"

"Who? Who? Spup, who's back?"

The commotion woke Hannah, who was now upset, crying for her mother. Elizabeth tried to soothe them both but was unsuccessful.

"The evil ones, they're chasing me, it's dark…they won't leave…they won't forgive me," Spupaleena said as

her trembling intensified. "They say I belong to them...
kunheet in ("Help Me")."

"Spupaleena, why won't they forgive you? What
happened? Please talk to me, Spupaleena," Elizabeth
begged.

"Loot, I can't, loot." Spupaleena's dark eyes were
filled with pain and confusion. She sobbed uncontrollably; hanging on to Elizabeth's arm with a grip so strong
she left a bruise.

Elizabeth peeled herself away from Spupaleena's
grip and stood, hurrying to gather and soothe her
flailing baby.

"It's time to confront them."

"Loot, they'll kill me," Spupaleena said, her voice
desperate.

"I'm going to pray for you, it will be alright, honey,
God's love is more powerful. He will take care of you;
you have to trust me—and him."

She prayed over Spupaleena, rebuking any evil that
was coming against the girl. She prayed with every
fiber in her body, asking God to release her friend of
the stronghold binding her, preventing a spiritual healing and not ceasing until the trembling completely left
her body. She did not stop until she felt God's peace
cover Spupaleena. She did not stop until she saw the
girl's body go limp. She prayed until they were both
exhausted. Elizabeth prayed for as long as it took.

Elizabeth noticed her baby had settled down as well. "Thank you, God." She kissed Hannah tenderly and placed her back in the cradle.

The weight of exhaustion was heavy, yet gratifying. This battle had been won. Victory, she knew, was not her own, but of the blood of Jesus. The cross fought the battle and the cross won.

Elizabeth ran her fingers through Spupaleena's hair. "Rest now, child, try and get some sleep," she whispered.

"I'm so tired," Spupaleena said. Her eyes barely open and she was dripping with sweat.

Elizabeth fetched a cool rag to rest on Spupaleena's forehead.

"I know, sleep peacefully," Elizabeth said. She sat down by the side of the bed, stroking the young girl's hair from the roots to the ends until Spupaleena fell asleep, looking so innocent. *What could she have ever done to think she never deserved any type of exoneration?* Elizabeth thought.

She picked up her baby and reclined in the rocker, pondering Spupaleena's dilemma. Looking down at Hannah, Elizabeth smiled, noticing how much she resembled her father. Smiling and satisfied, Elizabeth, now allowing herself to relax, rocked and hummed.

Hannah cooed quietly. "What a blessing you are to me. Your papa'll be so proud. You'll meet him soon, when God brings him home. You'll love him as much as I do." Elizabeth played with Hannah's long fingers.

"Your papa, he is gentle and strong. He'll be so excited to see your tiny face, to hold you in his arms," Elizabeth whispered, a tear trickling down her cheek. "I love you, Hannah."

Elizabeth rested her head against the back of the rocker, closed her eyes, and hummed one of her favorite hymns, one her mother loved. This time she hummed praising the Lord. Her mother had taught her and her siblings early on to praise God not only in the good and wonderful times, but also in the seasons of struggle.

She was soon asleep.

Chapter 11

It was early afternoon when Spupaleena opened her eyes. The room was dark and quiet. Blankets were hung over the two windows in the cabin. Besides the light from the fire, only one lantern was dimly flickering. She scanned the cabin to find Elizabeth at the table, searching through the pages of her Bible. Hannah was nestled asleep in her cradle. Spupaleena slid out of bed and limped over to the table. She sat down beside Elizabeth and let the silence stir the air.

"How do you feel?" Elizabeth asked, as she set her Bible aside. "Can I get you anything?"

After a few seconds, Spupaleena spoke. "I'm ready to forgive," she said matter-of-factly. "I want to be needed and loved. You have shown that to me—you and Phillip. I want to be free of the evil and hate inside me."

"You're doing the right thing," Elizabeth was caught off guard. She had prayed for so long and was now at a loss for words. They embraced, rocking back and forth, savoring the moment. Elizabeth prayed with Spupaleena to ask God for forgiveness and to come in and be the Lord of her life. With those words, an enormous burden of bitterness and resentment lifted from the girl. The hair stood on her neck and shivers danced down her spine.

"I'm so happy for you!" Elizabeth said.

"Lim lumt. I feel good…and relieved. I feel *inpee-eels* ("Happy")," Spupaleena said, struggling to find the right words to match her emotions.

"I bet you do. This is a good time as any if you want to know anything. Is there anything you'd like to talk about?"

"Kewa, I want to know a lot, like…why is God so forgiving? I'm glad he is, but why? We can be so mean and say such hurtful things."

"Why wouldn't he, Spupaleena?"

Elizabeth was a bit confused. She thought, perhaps only assumed, Spupaleena understood God's mercy better than she did. She stood as Spupaleena deliberated her answer and fetched them both some milk and a plate of cookies.

"Who is he, really?" Spupaleena asked softly. She reached for a cookie and took a bite.

"What do you mean?"

"I know he forgives us and loves us. But what is he like?" Spupaleena shrugged her shoulders. She had witnessed God's healing and faithfulness, but also realized she was unsure she truly comprehended who his person was.

Elizabeth walked to the fire, tossed a log on, and sat back down.

She sighed thoughtfully. "Well, God is someone who loves us all the time. He loves us when we follow him and he loves us when we go our own way." Elizabeth drank her milk and let the thought work its way into Spupaleena's heart. Elizabeth had prayed all morning that her friend would again open herself up to share her feelings, her past. Now that she had, Elizabeth sensed a strong urge to be cautious and not dig too deep, but to let the Holy Spirit lead her.

"What else?" Spupaleena said with a bit of eagerness in her voice.

"God is love. He created this world, including everything and everyone in it. He wants us to be happy and healthy. He wants us to love and trust in him every day in every situation."

"Tell me more about Jesus. Who were his parents?"

Elizabeth chuckled. "Well, Jesus is God's Son, the Creator's Son." She motioned to the sky. "His mother was a faithful daughter of the Lord—"

"What do you mean daughter?" Spupaleena interrupted.

"When we become Christians, we become sons and daughters of God…like adoption. We come into his family. It's our choice to do so really, but God loves us just like your stimteema loves you, no matter what."

Spupaleena's eyes brightened as she thought of her grandmother. "Was she like you and me or a spirit?" If its one thing she understood, it was the spirit world.

"She was like you and me, a human. Her name was Mary."

Spupaleena sat there in silence for some time. She looked from Elizabeth to the table, around the cabin, and back at Elizabeth. "You're telling me a spirit and a human made Jesus?" Spupaleena's eyes widened and her jaw dropped. She grew serious. "Here's what I was brought up to believe."

Elizabeth gave her full attention. Another story, she was eager to hear it.

"My people came from the Animal People. Young Wolf made the first person."

Spupaleena twisted to find a more comfortable spot in her chair. "Beaver's flesh was cut into twelve pieces, which were to become twelve people. The Animal People carried the flesh to different lands and shared their breath and removed any poison from the flesh. The Animal People showed the first twelve people where to find food and water, what roots were good, and where berries grew," Spupaleena shared.

"That's interesting. Tell me more."

"That's it!" Spupaleena raised her hands in finality.

"I see." Elizabeth nodded her head. This was not going as planned. She presumed Spupaleena would share more now that her life had been given over to the

Savior. Elizabeth decided to simply love her and accept who she was and to refrain from rushing progress.

Spupaleena needed to learn more about God. She had a strong craving to trust him, but she was hesitant. Trust was an issue for her. There were too many open wounds and she was unwilling to let walls of doubt come down. For the next several days, the girls read through different books of the Bible and discussed many of God's truths. Spupaleena was hungry for answers and discernment.

The days were longer and the worst of the winter cold was over. Spring and its unpredictability were welcoming.

Elizabeth had begun outlining her garden. She wanted to teach Spupaleena the basics, but was unsure of Spupaleena's future intentions. She had no idea if the girl would stay, move on, or try to return home. The latter seemed to be the least likely. Spupaleena was so young. Elizabeth hoped her beloved friend would stay on as long as possible—years if needed.

Elizabeth was sitting at the table, deep in garden planning when Spupaleena approached her.

"Elizabeth, do you like your sisters?" she said with caution.

"Yes, I love them very much." She smiled.

"Kewa, but are you friends with them?" She tilted her head to one side. "Do you like them?" She picked up a package of beans, not really paying attention to what they were.

Elizabeth set a pack of corn seeds by the pile of pea seeds. "Well, with six sisters, it's hard to get close to all of them. I suppose I'm closer to some more than others. Molly and I are the closest in age and the oldest, so it's easy to be the better of friends." She glanced up at Spupaleena. "We usually only had each other to play with because three of the boys came next."

"That would be so nice, to have a sister to play with and share dreams with." Spupaleena looked down at the floor.

"Yes, it was. But I also had a sister who said I, being the oldest, was bossy…very motherly." Elizabeth giggled. "She was eleven years younger than me." Elizabeth sat in her chair smiling at the memories of her tattle-tailing little sister. Those were memories she had not pulled forth in a long time.

"What was her name? Is she still alive?" Spupaleena asked eagerly.

"No, she's not." Elizabeth sighed. "She passed away when she was just eight years old. She died of pneumonia. She was so sick that day. I remember Mamma being so worried. She prayed all day. Then Lilian just gave up and went home. It was hard for Mamma to lose two little ones so early in life."

"Home, what do you mean?"

"Home, to be with the Lord," Elizabeth said, glancing up. "She went to live with God in heaven."

"Did you and your sisters hit each other, not just playing, but in a mean way?" Spupaleena paused, her eyes glaring and cold. Her look caught Elizabeth off guard.

"Heavens no, Spupaleena. I would get after the younger ones, even Molly would. We would spank them, but never beat them. No one would ever think of hurting the other," Elizabeth explained. She was stunned. She sat there, wondering if that was how she and Hamis-hamis interacted.

Spupaleena stood and walked over to the fire.

Elizabeth turned and watched her, searching for the right words. "I know you had hard times. I know your sister hurt you. I don't know much more, but I do know this, sisters aren't always mean. Mine were loving. They can be loving, Spupaleena."

Spupaleena grunted with disgust. She turned and held her gaze on Hannah, who was lying in her cradle. She was content. Spupaleena stood stiff, fighting off her pent-up anger. Even though she was now saved, she struggled to release the bitterness.

"Did other sisters fight in your village, like you and Hamis-hamis?"

Spupaleena shook her head slowly. "Loot."

"Then why are you holding such resentment?" Elizabeth was feeling that Spupaleena was keeping more than a few spats from her.

"What's troubling you, Spupaleena? Something happened that you aren't telling me. What is it?" Elizabeth's voice was soft and nurturing, yet inquiring.

Tears rolled down Spupaleena's face. "I…I can't." She suddenly hobbled as fast as she could out the door. Elizabeth was startled. Spupaleena's leg had healed enough that she was almost to the wooded area before Elizabeth got her wits about her and was able to scramble down the steps.

"Spupaleena," Elizabeth screamed after her. Cupping her hands over her mouth, she shouted again. "Spupaleena!" She wanted to run after her but had to stay with the baby.

Elizabeth had to let Spupaleena go, praying her friend would come back soon. She trembled at the sight of the girl disappearing into the forest. She needed to know what Spupaleena was hiding. The girl was running from something that hurt too profoundly—enough to run away in the middle of a winter blizzard and nearly freeze to death.

Spupaleena ran. She ran until she could no longer withstand the pain in her leg. Her chest was heaving from running so fast. She was back where she started, running away—running from her past, running and broken. Spupaleena slowed to a stop and searched the terrain. She had a hard time recognizing where she was. She circled once and toppled back, hitting the now thawing earth with a thud. She couldn't think, nor did she care to.

Carmen Peone

The moon was barely showing and the mountains hid the sun. Sweat ran down Spupaleena's brow. Her lungs burned and she was unable to move. She closed her bloodshot eyes, curling up into a ball.

An owl making its presence known caught Spupaleena's attention.

She gasped. "Death will surely come." The messenger of blackness came to announce the truth of her pathetic life. *Sneena* ("Owl") had come to sentence her. No one could save her now. Spupaleena rolled over onto her stomach and planted her face in her arms, accepting her fate. She felt no pain. She felt nothing.

Moment's later, sneena called to her again, almost by name. She thought she was hearing things. Suddenly, she felt a deep urge to pray. She began singing a prayer song her grandmother had taught her early on. The sound came from deep within her throat, from years of guilt and shame.

"God, show yourself to me. Show me that I'm forgiven as Elizabeth tells me I am. I need you now, God. Show your face to me!" she begged.

Late into the night, Spupaleena rose and danced in circle after circle. She danced around trees, plants, and shrubs, not noticing the cold or the sounds of the stirring creatures beginning to awaken. She sang and danced with a limpness to her stride and groaning passion in her voice. When the sun peeked over the mountains, Spupaleena was still swaying to her own beat—a pulse that kept one foot tapping in front of the other.

Her head and body still hung limp with fatigue. She was deep in prayer. But at least now, she had an answer. God was faithful, and there would be no more death. Sneena was mistaken.

Elizabeth was already up and dressed. The fire roared and the cabin was finally warming up. She paced the floor humming.

"Spupaleena should have been back by now," she mumbled.

She poured a third cup of coffee so strong it would cause any mountain man to sweat. Elizabeth turned her head to Hannah as she stirred in her crib. She hoped the child would sleep a little while longer. Too many scenarios were swirling in her head that needed all of her attention. Elizabeth was beat. She hardly slept, which was evident by the dark circles under her eyes.

"Oh Lord, heavenly Father, please let Spupaleena be somewhere warm and unharmed. Could she have found proper shelter through the night?" Elizabeth dropped her head into her shaking hands. She paced in between fervent prayer. Fits of sleep fell upon her here and there that morning, but was never enough. She was thankful Hannah had slept soundly.

A crackling sound caught her attention, it was coming from outside. Elizabeth flew to the door. She opened it and stuck her head outside, not noticing the freezing air swirling about her nor the frost on the ground. She studied the landscape, searching for even the tiniest clue as to the sound, hoping it would be her friend coming home. She saw nothing. "Lord, please..." she whispered.

Elizabeth closed the door and sat down. Her heart was pounding. She sipped her coffee and then placed the cup on the kitchen table. There was nothing she could do but continue to wait and trust.

Elizabeth stoked the fire and tried to accomplish something, making the time pass. She thought, *Would Spupaleena try to come home soon, or was she gone forever? Would she move on and really not tell Elizabeth of her plans? Would she not even say good-bye?*

Spupaleena came up on the cabin ready to face Elizabeth with a renewed assurance. She was sorry about running away like she had, but knew going home and facing her fears was the right thing to do. She was walking taller with less of a limp, tired of feeling sorry for herself.

The afternoon sun massaged her head and back like warm fingers. Yes, Spupaleena felt confident to begin her journey. First, she must settle her affairs with Elizabeth, her dear sister.

She approached the door and placed her hand on the handle, saying a quick prayer while pushing the door open. Odd was the silence. Still holding the handle, she shook her head and peered in as her eyes adjusted to the darkness. Sighing with relief, she saw Elizabeth fast asleep in her rocker with her sewing on her lap. Her eyes followed the room to the cradle were Hannah was also sleeping.

"Spupaleena!" She clasped her hands. "Thank the Lord you're all right," Elizabeth whispered sleepily. Shifting in her chair, she placed her sewing on the table and walked to her beloved friend, embracing her with a silent prayer of thanksgiving.

"Elizabeth, I have something I must tell you," Spupaleena said hesitantly.

"Yes, but first let's eat. You must be starving. Out all night…" Elizabeth was still shook up. "We'll eat and then you can tell me all about your night."

Spupaleena nodded in agreement and sat down. Hannah began to stir, so Spupaleena tended to her while Elizabeth whipped up some fried potatoes with biscuits and gravy. She hummed as she worked, this time with relief and praise.

Chapter 12

Elizabeth had been beside herself throughout the night, running on little sleep. She finally had peace now that Spupaleena was home and safe. She sensed a renewed spirit in Spupaleena, but realized she needed to wait until her friend made the first move to discuss the past evening's events.

"I've been so worried," Elizabeth said, sitting, wringing her hands in her lap.

"I know, my <u>l</u>thkickha. I'm sorry I scared you," Spupaleena said slowly, her eyes downcast.

"I—"

"Please, let me say what's in my heart." Spupaleena interrupted with such tenderness.

"Yes, go on..." Elizabeth heard Hannah fuss. She went and grabbed her, taking care of her needs.

"I'm sorry." Spupaleena took a drink of water. "I shouldn't have run out like I did...I...I was wrong and selfish."

Elizabeth waited a moment before she spoke. "Yes, it was wrong, you frightened me, but I love you, Spupaleena. I forgive you. That's what friends and family do...love, share, forgive," Elizabeth explained. She gazed softly and caringly at Spupaleena.

"Kewa, and I love you. I need to tell you about last night," Spupaleena said. Her face brightened and a huge smile broke out on her golden-brown face. This reaction puzzled Elizabeth. She had never witnessed Spupaleena this confident.

"I was lying on the cold, wet earth not knowing whether to run away or come back here. I was hungry and chilled; anger filled my whole body. I barely felt anything. I could have cared less. My arms and legs hardly moved..." Spupaleena's eyes were big and bright.

"Something told me to pray like never before. I started to sing a song my grandmother taught me when I was young. The song asked for power, for wisdom and courage," Spupaleena rocked back and forth as she spoke.

"But—" Spupaleena held her hand out in front of her, shaking her head.

"I cried out to the Creator, yours and mine. I sang and prayed all night. When the sun came up over the mountains, my decision was made." Spupaleena sat quietly staring at the floor. How could she tell her new-found sister she needed to go away? God was calling her home, to reconcile with her family.

Beads of sweat trickled down the sides of Elizabeth's face, knowing what was coming. She felt faint. She looked up at Spupaleena with a false sense of calm and asked her to continue.

Spupaleena could see the fear in Elizabeth's eyes. She could feel the mood change. Spupaleena needed to put her beloved friend at ease, but was unsure how.

"Elizabeth…" Spupaleena walked over and knelt on the floor facing her friend. She placed Elizabeth's hands in her own. "You have been so good to me, like family—a <u>lth</u>kickha." She chuckled. "At times a mother."

Spupaleena stroked the baby's soft head. "You have helped me heal my wounds with your good medicine and helped me heal inside with your God medicine. Lim lumt."

Elizabeth nodded in humility. She swallowed and allowed a tear to roll down her flushed cheek.

"I have a story to tell you," Spupaleena sat on the floor, placing her hands on her lap. She took a deep breath.

Elizabeth gave Spupaleena her full attention, now that Hannah was fast asleep.

"I want to share how I feel." She paused, putting her thoughts in order, unsure of how to begin. "Before I came here, before my accident, I felt like a horse that was tethered all the time. I was controlled and not allowed to run free like I was created to do. Only with my mistum did I feel cut loose. I was tethered and sad.

I would ask for food and shelter, but was only whipped and shouted at," Spupaleena whispered, her voice breaking. She fought back the tears. Her mouth was dry, suddenly she felt self-conscious. She mustered up the courage to continue.

"I was given some food and water, enough to survive, but my heart was wounded, I was always on guard to the predators surrounding me…waiting for the slap on my head, to be yelled at and worked, and always tethered. Rocks were thrown at me by some of my family and others in the herd. I hurt inside, some days it felt hard to breathe. I cried a lot when I was alone."

Elizabeth understood Spupaleena's interpretation, feeling her pain. She hated to see her friend reliving her agony. She sent her a prayer of strength and comfort.

"I wanted to break loose, to break free from the rope that held me captive. I felt my brother's death was my fault and I wasn't strong enough to loosen the chokehold it had on me." Spupaleena took a sip of water, pausing to finger her cup. "One day, I did get my chance. I was tied loosely and broke the line. I ran hard and fast. I galloped off at dangerously high speeds. I was angry and frantic—wild-eyed, but at the same time, it didn't matter because I was finally free." Relief showered Spupaleena's face and her eyes shimmered in the glow of the fire.

Elizabeth sat, taking in every word and emotion. She wished she could soothe and hold Spupaleena the way she did with Hannah.

"I ran wildly, not noticing where I was going, not even caring. I felt release and that's all that mattered. I felt light and unbound. I continued to run uncontrollably, not paying attention to where I was going. In the snow, I slipped and tumbled down an icy ravine. I was badly hurt, scared, and lonely."

Spupaleena slowed down and spoke softly and purposefully. "Then, a man came and rescued me. He brought me to a woman and a barn. The barn was warm with fresh straw. The woman, his wife, had great healing powers. She brushed me and fed me fresh green hay. I had plenty of water. Eventually, my body healed...the woman took such good care of me. She tossed a carrot my way on occasion." Spupaleena broke out into a wide grin. She flashed her a look of admiration.

"She loved me just for the horse I was. She cared less if I had spots or none at all. It didn't matter that I was skinny, showing my bones through my hide. I was hurt and mangled; it just made no difference to her." Spupaleena reached out to hold Elizabeth's hand. "My mane was in knots and my coat was thick with muck, but she still loved me for who I was."

"So now what?" Elizabeth mopped her damp forehead with her sleeve.

"I owe my life to you and Phillip. But now my <u>lth-kickha</u>, I must go. I must face my hurt and fears...my family…Hamis-hamis." Spupaleena's voice cracked, she could hardly get the words to come out. Her eyes searched Elizabeth's for some kind of response. All Elizabeth could do was weep. Spupaleena got on her knees, reaching up for Elizabeth. They held on to each other for several precious moments.

They pulled apart, but continued to hold hands. "God has shown me that I need to put my hurts behind me and forgive, to make amends with Hamis-hamis and my toom. I must let them know that I am alive and well."

"But how will you travel? How will you find your way? And what were you talking about…your dead brother? I thought he was alive!"

Spupaleena nodded.

"Kewa, I know the way." She stood and walked to her bed. She pulled a rolled up hide out from under her blanket.

Elizabeth sighed, holding out her hands. "How?" she asked anxiously.

"Phillip told me exactly where he found me, when you were sleeping. He told me before he left, drawing me a map on this old cow skin. I begged him to show me before he left for Lincoln." She handed Elizabeth the tattered hide.

"But, can you really find your way home?" Elizabeth protested, rising up out of her chair as if it were red hot.

"Kewa, with the help of the Creator. He gave me a vision last night—the way home." Spupaleena's heart felt like it would beat right out of her chest. She wrung her sweaty hands. "Now, there is more I have to tell you," she said, gesturing toward Elizabeth's rocker.

"More? Don't know if I can take more." She tossed the hide aside.

Still unnerved, Elizabeth took her cue and sat back down. She rocked her chair with anticipation. What more could Spupaleena possible have to say. *She's already bent on trying to find her own way home, a single, young girl—a recipe for trouble,* she thought. Elizabeth's face became flush and she rocked even more rapidly, fanning herself with a tin plate. Spupaleena took her place back on the floor.

Hannah stirred in her cradle. Elizabeth resisted the urge to go pick her up. The baby examined her mother, smiling and cooing, not a care in the world and oblivious to the tension swirling around her mother. Elizabeth could only share a counterfeit smile.

Spupaleena drew in a big breath and released her anxiety slowly and deeply. Elizabeth's attention returned to her friend, who calmly continued her story.

"When Hamis-hamis and I were younger, we had a baby brother, another one. Our toom told us to fetch water down by the creek and to take him with us. His name was **Kook Yuma May Ooya** ("Little Raccoon"). He had just learned to walk," Spupaleena said with a forced smile. Guilt robbed her of the ability to enjoy the happy memories she had left of him. "Hamis-hamis and I argued the whole way to the river. I have no idea why, nor does it matter. We weren't paying attention to our brother…"

Spupaleena folded her arms over her belly allowing a tear to escape. "He wandered into the river," she whispered. Her throat felt constricted; her breathing was shallow. She took a drink of water then placed the cup on the floor. She shook her head in disbelief. "What had we done?" She looked up at Elizabeth, tears pooling in her eyes. "What had we done? He was fearless, and we weren't paying attention to him. We knew better."

Elizabeth leaned forward, placing her hands gently on Spupaleena's shoulders, and prayed. "Precious Lord, let your comfort wrap its arms around Spupaleena, cover her with your blanket of peace and favor; let her come safely into your dwelling place," she whispered.

Elizabeth knew there were no words that could take away the years of hurt and loss. She wondered how much time Spupaleena had lived with torment and bitterness. This was the kind that cut straight through a person's heart and soul leaving not even a crumb of hope behind.

"Nothing you can do could ever take away my love for you—nor God's. It was an accident; it was an accident," Elizabeth whispered. She held on to Spupaleena and stroked her hair in a gentle, motherly way.

"Hamis-hamis has blamed me all these years… so had my toom. I was the one watching him while

Carmen Peone

Hamis-hamis filled the water buckets," she said, her voice tight. "I was the one paying attention to my own anger and not my brother." Spupaleena wept so hard her eyes swelled and she felt nauseous.

"Still, no one is to blame, you were both in charge of watching him, it's not your fault," Elizabeth replied. "Just as it was an accident that my baby died, no one is held responsible. It was his time to go home to be with God; it was your little brother's time to go home as well."

"But it still hurts—" The tension in her throat rendered her words to a whisper.

"Yes, but your hurt will heal, it will, I promise."

Elizabeth held on to Spupaleena for a long time. This was the first time Spupaleena had ever talked about her deceased brother. Elizabeth rocked her back and forth, praying over her and crying with her. Many tears came with their friendship, but most were tears of healing, tears to wash the inside as a bath washes the outside.

"Will God really take my pain away?" Spupaleena sniffed, grabbing a cool, wet rag to wipe her nose and face.

Nodding slowly, Elizabeth answered. "Yes, he will, in time. But you have to let him. I know it's hard, but releasing your hurt and anger to God will wash the pain away, it just takes awhile sometimes. You will never forget, but you will go on, living and dreaming as God takes you from one situation or blessing to another. Life continues on and we become stronger and wiser."

Rubbing her forehead, Spupaleena agreed. "Kewa, I understand. I know I've been forgiven, but I also must forgive Hamis-hamis…as God has forgiven me. He shared that with me last night. Believing can be hard sometimes." She sat and stared at her empty glass.

Elizabeth pushed a wisp of hair off Spupaleena's forehead and smiled. "Yes it can. God never said it would be easy, just that he would walk through life with us and never leave. He delights in blessing us and he also sheds his tears when we hurt." She glanced over at her fussy baby. "You also have to forgive yourself."

Spupaleena nodded.

Elizabeth went and gathered the red-faced Hannah up out of her bed to change her cloth diaper. She was voicing her discomfort quite loudly. "I agree you need to forgive and am thankful you recognize the need to do so, or I'm afraid the bitterness will only continue to fester and destroy your joy. God wants us to live a happy life, having the ability to heal inside," Elizabeth assured her. "I have learned through the years that he is a God of restoration."

Elizabeth laid the baby on her bed, reaching for a clean cloth and pins. She changed the soiled diaper and handed her to Spupaleena. "Sometimes, I feel strong, yet at other times, I feel so weak…and—"

"And you will. That's where we just have to give our worries and heart to Jesus and let him do the rest."

Chapter 13

"Today I begin my new journey!" Spupaleena announced.

She had woke up feeling bright and confident. A sense of release encouraged her after she finally revealed her shame-filled secret. Forgiveness gave her a lightness, which brought with it security and assurance. She believed her decision to return home was the right path to walk.

After lying in bed longer than needed, Spupaleena got up and dressed for the day. She knew Elizabeth would have more questions, and she refused to leave with matters unresolved.

Elizabeth slept fitfully during the night. Even Hannah was restless. Elizabeth believed the little one could sense the strained emotions running throughout her mother. But Hannah was a comfort in the late of the night.

The smell of eggs and ham filled the room. Elizabeth was up early and picking up last night's mending. She mumbled to herself in between attempts to hum, "Where He Leads, I will Follow."

She tried to read out of the Book of Jeremiah that morning, but struggled as the words slipped out of her mind. She read Jeremiah over and over, but nothing seemed to stick. Good thing she had 29:11 memorized. "For I know the plans I have for you, declares the Lord, plans to prosper you and not harm you, plans to give you hope and a future." Elizabeth repeated those words over and over, if for nothing but comfort. She knew Spupaleena had the right to a future with her family. She had never really admitted to herself that someday Spupaleena would be gone.

"Spupaleena." Elizabeth, somewhat agitated, glanced in her direction as the girl sat by the fire, drinking her morning tea. Spupaleena watched Elizabeth flitter around the house like a hummingbird on a mission. "There is another horse in the corral with Sammy; do you know anything about that?" Elizabeth asked.

"Kewa," she replied, nodding her head. "I saw your neighbor…Mr…"

"Mr. Dalley?"

"Kewa, he put the horse in the corral last night and fed him too." She tried to hide her excitement, her very own horse.

"I see." Elizabeth replied. She knew something was up, but was in the dark.

"What's going on, may I ask?" Her faced was flushed, not by the intense heat of the cabin, but by the boiling anger rising inside her. This was the second time Spupaleena knew something that was obviously hidden from Elizabeth. *Why was Spupaleena hiding secrets? Why did Phillip and Jack keep maps and give horses—withholding all of this from me?* She thought.

"Uh, I, uh, awhile back, Mr. Dalley came and gave her to me, well, he said I could have her for the journey home. He made sure I had her…" Her voice dropped. She could see the disappointment written all over Elizabeth's face.

Elizabeth threw her hands into the air. "And where was I?"

"You were sleeping. I was out feeding Sammy and… he didn't want to wake you."

"I see." Elizabeth felt betrayed.

"He told me then—"

"And when was I to know?" she interrupted.

"It wasn't time. I didn't want to upset you," Spupaleena pleaded. She was telling the truth and had not lied, just delayed the news until the right time came, which apparently was not now.

"You haven't even ridden—"

"Kewa, I have." Spupaleena nodded.

Elizabeth wiped her hands and threw her hand towel on the counter. "What?"

"Kewa, Mr. Dalley let me ride Sammy first, and then Rainbow."

"You rode Sammy and Rainbow?" Elizabeth's mouth twisted as the horse's name rolled off her tongue.

"Kewa, Rainbow, the mare's name, isn't she beautiful?" Spupaleena's eyes glistened with pride. Her smile melted Elizabeth's heart in mere seconds. "She's really gentle." Spupaleena pleaded her case.

Her anger dissipated as quickly as fog in the sunshine.

Elizabeth chuckled, she could never be mad at Spupaleena for very long. She knew there was no stopping the girl. Who could be upset when Spupaleena was so excited, she was instantly horse-crazy once she discovered Sammy. She remembers the day; Spupaleena relentlessly pestered Phillip about the gelding.

"So Jack gave you riding lessons? Why I didn't wake up with all that commotion is beyond me."

"It was the day after Hannah was up all night with… with the sick belly?"

"Yes, colic," Elizabeth giggled.

"So you know your way home, huh?"

"Kewa, I'll show you," Spupaleena said. She reached for the map Phillip had sketched out for her.

"What is this?" Elizabeth said, as she reached for the cow hide. "Oh, yes, the map." Elizabeth said sarcastically. She vaguely remembered tossing it aside the previous day.

"A map of directions for my journey home," Spupaleena said, trying to keep the mood cheerful.

Elizabeth studied the detailed directions. She nodded her head in amazement. "These look very accurate. I can't believe it," she stated. "I should have known."

"With God's help, and the help of my animal friend, I'm surely able to make it home," Spupaleena said enthusiastically.

"I see." Elizabeth sighed. She handed the map back to Spupaleena and went to her bed. She sat down, her body trembling. She was fearful for her new little sister. Just a child she was, really. "When will you go?"

"I will leave in the morning, at first light," Spupaleena whispered. The laughter they had just shared faded with the morning chill.

Elizabeth could only nod. She looked at Spupaleena and then at Hannah. She lay down and gazed at the ceiling. She felt helpless and empty. *I should have known this day would come*, she thought. She closed her eyes, knowing she had to let Spupaleena go.

The sun was not yet up when Spupaleena rose out of her warm, cozy bed. She had been restless under the quilts. Remembering the sorrow in Elizabeth's eyes was enough to tempt her to stay. She heard Elizabeth weep off and on throughout the night. After a while of reflection, she finally got up and went to Hannah's crib, memorizing every detail on her tiny pink face and body. Leaning over the side of the crib, Spupaleena whispered a prayer of health and strength as the child grew in age.

Spupaleena drew Hannah's tiny hand into her own and brushed her lips across her tiny fingers, soaking in the warmth. She softly kissed the chubby little hand, taking in a deep breath, and then gently placed it back under the soft blanket, not wanting to wake the baby up. She attempted to hold back her tears. She felt the lump in her throat, almost choking. As she slowly released the trapped air in her lungs, the tears burst as quickly as a broken water dam. Spupaleena loved Hannah deeply, making her miss her own brother. She longed to hold him again and wondered how big Pekam was now.

"Grow up strong, precious little Hannah," she whispered, holding her tiny fingers.

Spupaleena let go and sobbed, nearly waking Elizabeth. She stood only for a moment over the cradle—it was time to leave. She declined to face Elizabeth a second time. Her heart would shatter. She gathered her belongings and some food, quietly sneaking out of the cabin. She climbed on her sorrel mare and walked quietly to the edge of the woods. Sammy nickered as if to say good-bye. She stopped and turned her head.

"I will see you again." She bowed her head in prayer. She prayed for wisdom and strength for her expedition home, including safety and health for Elizabeth, Phillip, and Hannah. She turned her mare, giving her a gentle squeeze, and clucked her tongue. Lifting her chin, they walked forward. Spupaleena was on the final leg of her passage to forgiveness. She had a change of heart. She looked forward to this new path in life, putting the past behind her. She longed for her mistum and stimteema. She longed for love and acceptance. She prayed for her family as she traveled through the woods.

"Thank you, Lord God, for taking care of me, for healing my wounds. Prepare me for what's to come, for the family that waits for my return. Soften their hearts so we may come together as a family through your love. Thank you for this new journey," Spupaleena said. She was ready to face what lay ahead of her. She had serenity. She had God.

listen|imagine|view|experience

AUDIO BOOK DOWNLOAD INCLUDED WITH THIS BOOK!

In your hands you hold a complete digital entertainment package. In addition to the paper version, you receive a free download of the audio version of this book. Simply use the code listed below when visiting our website. Once downloaded to your computer, you can listen to the book through your computer's speakers, burn it to an audio CD or save the file to your portable music device (such as Apple's popular iPod) and listen on the go!

How to get your free audio book digital download:

1. Visit www.tatepublishing.com and click on the e|LIVE logo on the home page.
2. Enter the following coupon code:
   c577-ceb7-25b0-d529-bf86-4e1d-b225-2a56
3. Download the audio book from your e|LIVE digital locker and begin enjoying your new digital entertainment package today!